A BAD BOY BILLIONAIRE ROMANCE

LINNEA MAY

ISBN-13: 978-1541319592
ISBN-10: 1541319591

Kingston

She tries to evade my touch, but I'm faster than her – and more resolute.

There's no denying it. She can act and pretend all she wants, but I know that she wants me to touch her. Every fiber of her being is calling out to me, begging me to take her.

I have her cornered and am pushing her back against the wall with just the intensity of my sheer presence, placing my hand right next to her pretty face and thus blocking her escape. We're alone, she's at my mercy, and for a few blessed moments, I can do whatever I want to her, whatever both of us want to happen.

Her green eyes wander up timidly to meet mine. I can see they're filled with fear – and lust. She's afraid of her own desires, because she knows it's wrong. This isn't supposed to happen.

And yet it will.

"Please let me go," she pleads, her voice so soft that it's barely audible.

Her eye fixate on mine, contradicting her words.

"I will," I promise. "After I've tasted those pretty lips of yours."

Her eyes widen and a somber sigh escapes her lips when I touch them with my thumb.

"Please," she whispers. "We can't..."

That's just the thing I want to hear.

We can't.

We shouldn't.

This isn't right.

I like a good challenge, and that's why I like girls like her. The more there is to overcome, the more I want them. Her weak attempts at fending me off, combined with those pleading eyes, it's making it impossible for me to resist.

She is the most forbidden fruit ever to tease me. I want her, and I always get what I want.

Her breasts are heaving under her heavy, gaspy breathing. She's clasping her music sheets against her chest as if they can protect her from me.

I lean down, moving my face closer to hers, so close until I can feel her breath on my lips.

"Please," she pleads.

"Please, what?" I ask, knowing that she won't be able to reply.

My fingers wander along her feminine jaw line, barely touching her skin as I travel down to her neck. I want to close my hand around that slim neck and choke her.

What would she do? Would she enjoy it? Would she faint from the climax that could come with it?

My cock twitches against my zipper at the thought of it. It will be a while until I get to test her, but the wait will be worth it.

But for now, I need to be patient. She's not going to be an easy one to claim.

And she still hasn't given me a verbal reply. However, her big green eyes tell me everything I need to know, as my finger tips trail seductively along her collar bone.

I don't ask for permission – I never do – but she's giving it to me anyway.

There's no protest. She doesn't try to fight or stop me when I lean in even closer. A suffocated moan is all I hear when our lips finally meet and my tongue invades her mouth.

She reciprocates, breathing faster as our tongues intertwine in a wild and hungry dance. Her moaning adds to the symphony of our first kiss, and when she starts squirming towards me, I almost lose it.

My hand finds its way behind her back and as I pull her body closer to mine, she lets go of the sheets of music. They float down to the floor, spreading around our feet, as her hands fly up to embrace me. She's too short, but I realize her intentions. She tries to reach the back of my head and grab my hair.

That's not going to happen. I'm in control, and the sooner she learns this, the better.

I want to grab her wrists and push them down, but for now, I prefer to feel her dainty body pressed needily against mine.

CHAPTER I

Elodie

This is the opportunity of a lifetime.

For once, Lady Luck has picked me. I still can't believe it, but as I walk out the doors of the main building of Juilliard to cross over the bridge to my dorm, the realization slowly settles in.

I got it! I got chosen for one of the best gigs that have been posted since I started applying for paid performances. Of course, I've played at various occasions before, and been paid before, too, but never this much. The salary for this job is not only ridiculously high to begin with, but it also comes with a promise for more opportunities like it.

I have been asked to play at an engagement party being hosted by two old money families on the Upper East Side. If everything goes well and they like my playing, this gig will lead to more – the rehearsal dinner, the wedding and who knows what other associated events might need a piano accompaniment.

It's perfect. When two spoiled kids get hitched on a scale like this, their families will makes sure everybody and their brother attends. I will play in front of hundreds of wealthy guests who hold occasions like this on a regular basis. Dinner parties, more weddings, birthdays, reunions. If they like the pianist who performed at the Abrams-Waldorf wedding, it's the equivalent of a glowing recommendation and they're likely going to ask the families for the pianist's contact information.

And that pianist would be me.

Never in my wildest dreams have I dreamt of performing at such a large-scale event with so much potential. After all, I'm still a student, and it's unusual for students to be hired for an event like this. But the Abrams family specifically requested a student, for whatever reason. There are not that many second-year graduate students in the piano program at Juilliard, but I was still dumbfounded when our instructor, Mrs. Bellamy, approached me with the proposal.

"They asked specifically for a classical repertoire with some contemporary interpretations," she said. "And I believe you're the best choice."

I just stared at her, sitting on my hands and trying to process the magnitude of the winning lottery ticket that had just been handed to me.

"What do they mean by contemporary interpretations?" I asked her.

Mrs. Bellamy just shrugged. "You'll have to ask them yourself when you meet them."

That was about a week ago, and I'm scheduled to meet up with the family tonight. Mrs. Bellamy let them know that she had found someone, and they asked to meet with me as soon as possible. I've been nervous ever since, and subsequently made sure to add a few extra hours to my already full practice schedule. My scholarship only covers school tuition, and since I'm not as privileged as most of my fellow students, I had to take on a part-time job at one of the school's cafés to cover my living expenses. Having to work in addition to going to school and doing homework cuts down tremendously on the amount of time I have available to practice, but there's nothing I can do about it. I knew it wouldn't be easy.

I hate being poor. Who wouldn't? Poverty has always been a constant part of my life. One would think that I would have grown accustomed to it, since I don't know any different. But it's one thing to be poor when you're still living in your little microcosm across the river in Brooklyn, and it's something else entirely when you're plopped down in the middle of privileged society. Everybody was poor where I grew up, we were all the same, even though the degree of poverty varied. I grew up in an area that most people from Manhattan would not dare step foot in, let alone take a stroll at night, and I never liked it there. I wanted to get out as soon as possible, and I had a dream of how I was going to do it. I've had that dream ever since I was seven years old and found a tutor who was willing to take me under his wing, even though my father couldn't afford to pay the full amount he charged for piano lessons. Having that dream made me an outlier in school, but I was never treated any differently for it. We were all in the same boat, and I'm sure there were quite a few others who secretly dreamed of moving on to a life in Manhattan.

Only my dream wasn't to live in Manhattan, per se. My dream was and is to become a solo pianist. A solo pianist who can make a living with just her art. I know how farfetched that dream is, but I also knew that Juilliard would bring me closer to achieving that dream, a lot closer. Getting accepted at Juilliard was my number one goal all through junior high and high school.

And I made it.

But here at Juilliard, I'm an anomaly. I couldn't even attend this school if I hadn't been awarded enough scholarships to cover the cost of my tuition, but even with that and the part time jobs I've been taking, I can barely keep my head above water. New York is too expensive. I'm one of the very few graduate students who still live in the dorms. Most students choose to live off-campus once they finish their undergraduate studies. Graduate students, especially those in their second year, are a rarity here in campus housing.

Unfortunately, one of them is my roommate and regrettable three-night-stand Benjamin. Our paths cross as often as one would expect with two people living right next to each other, and even though it's been weeks since our last interlude, it doesn't get any less awkward. He's waiting to take the elevator up to our floor when I enter the building. We make eye contact before I can turn around and hide from him until he's gone to avoid an unpleasant encounter.

I come to a halt next to him and cast a smile his way. "Hi."

"Hello," he replies, his tone revealing how little he thinks of me.

I stare ahead at the elevator door and roll my eyes, oblivious to him. He's studying at the Juilliard School of Drama and the career path suits him so well.

There are eight people living in our simple suite on the 27th floor, and Benjamin's single room is right next to my double room. People warned me that hooking up with one of your roommates is probably one of the worst ideas ever. Of course it is. But it's easy to forget these things when you're drunk and just looking for some fun and a distracting hook-up.

I didn't think much of it at the time. I thought Benjamin of all people would understand that dating comes secondary in our current situation, especially when you're me. I simply don't have the time to build and maintain a relationship between all of my classes, hours of practice and part-time jobs, but I'm not *frigid*. It's only human to seek this kind of intimacy once in a while, even when the sex isn't really all that great or special.

I regret my hook-up with Benjamin on more than one level. It's not only the repercussions that annoy me, it's also the fact that the sex was so vanilla. Again and again I tell myself that I'd rather have no sex than bad sex. But how was I supposed to know that beforehand? Benjamin appears tough and masculine in public. How could I know that he turns into an awkward little puppy in the bedroom?

My biggest mistake was to repeat our drunken adventure again and again. For whatever reason, having sex more than twice made him believe that we went from being roommates to becoming a couple. I have no idea why he would think that, we weren't even that close before we slept together and we never grew any closer after we started hooking up.

The ice cold silence that surrounds us as we share the elevator upstairs is almost unbearable, so I decide to replace it with idle conversation.

"How is your play going?" I ask, knowing that he's currently working on a major part in an upcoming performance

"Good," he says, his voice stern. "Heard things are going quite well for you, too?"

I turn to look at him, but he evades my eyes.

"You heard about the Abrams-Waldorf engagement?" I ask him, thoroughly surprised.

He nods, and glances at me from the side. "Yes. Kim told me. Congratulations."

I know that his congratulations are not sincere, but I don't waste much thought on it.

"Thank you," I say, nonetheless. "I'm meeting up with them tonight. I really hope they'll hire me for the wedding, too."

We reach our floor and the elevator doors open, freeing us from our unpleasant confinement.

"Well, good for you," Benjamin snorts, as he strides through the door of our suite.

CHAPTER II

Kingston

I watch as Gloria twists a strand of her platinum blond hair between her fingers, absentmindedly staring at her phone through her thick fake eyelashes. She's sitting across the drawing room from me with her legs crossed, dressed in a sharp beige new women's suit that I've never seen on her before. I wouldn't be surprised if she bought it just for this meeting. Her earrings and matching necklace, both in that heavy gold tone I hate so much, also look new to me. Her thin lips are painted a deep red, matching her strong eye makeup and the rouge on her young cheeks, making her look so much older than she is.

Gloria is only 25 years old, but today her hair is styled like that of a middle-aged high society lady. Too similar to our mother's hair. It looks fucking ridiculous, and I know she only does it to please our stuck-up families.

She's playing a game. We both are. But she's so much better at this than I am.

"Don't you think we should be sitting next to each other?" she says, without looking up from her phone.

I huff. "I doubt it'll make a difference."

She looks up, piercing me with her steel blue eyes.

"I think it does," she hisses. "*Fiancé*."

She pats on the cushions next to her, inviting me to sit beside her as if I was a trained puppy.

I glare at her without moving an inch from my armchair on the other side of the seating area. This whole arrangement is ridiculous enough as it is, I won't make it any more believable by sitting next to the woman I'm supposed to marry per my parents' wishes. They both know that I don't care for Gloria the way a man should care for his wife-to-be – and it doesn't matter to them.

"It worked for us," they keep saying. Marriage is not much more than a business agreement in their eyes, and in the eyes of the circles in which my family socializes. This is all the more true for firstborns like me. My younger brother fled to the West Coast when he started college, that lucky bastard. The responsibility is not his to take on, and he pretty much gets to do whatever he pleases over there.

It's all on me. The main heir, my father's successor to the family empire.

I wouldn't be doing this if my parents hadn't threatened to take this position away from me. They've been pestering me to settle down and lose my promiscuous ways ever since I graduated from college and became CEO of one of our family's shipping companies. I'm good at what I do, and I enjoy being the boss. The way I see it, I'm not only able to continue the company's success, but make it even greater, because unlike my aging father, I'm capable of changing with the times. Things have changed, even in our traditional and century-old business, but he doesn't understand most of these changes. It's hurtful to the company, but every time I bring it up in front of him, he gets enraged.

I can't have our fortune destroyed by old man failures, but he refused to give me full control unless I'm willing to get married, settle down, and produce family heirs.

So, here we are. Gloria Waldorf and me. We've known each other since childhood, and she's one of the few women in my social circle who I've never hooked up with. That's how much I loathe that woman. She's superficial, manipulative, and there's not a single likable thing about her personality. She's shallow, and her snootiness and nosiness leads her to get involved in other people's business. Everything she says is either gossip, spiteful comments, or commands, because she's used to being served and treated like a princess. She always gets what she wants, and that includes a number of men. That may be the only thing we have in common, the promiscuity.

It may be surprising that nothing ever happened between us, even after our engagement was announced. However, next to my dislike for her, we also grew up together, which makes her seem more like a hated sister to me. Also, I'm simply not attracted to her with her excessive jewelry, the fake lashes, and the dyed platinum blond hair. The worst thing is that she smells like my mother because they both bathe in a similarly obtrusive stench of flowery perfume every day.

Yet, all of that makes her perfect to become my wife.

I know love is not for me. I haven't worked on my body this hard to be locked up in a cage, allowed to have just one woman for the rest of my life. I'm a player, and I have my looks and my wealth working for me. It's almost too easy sometimes because girls are easy. They all want the same thing, and I can give it to them. Three nights, three fucks, and never sleeping in the same bed - those are my limits. After that, I'm done with them. Always. I don't care if they're not done with me, but a few dodged phone calls usually gets the message across.

Seeing as neither Gloria nor I are in this for the love and the hellhole that's monogamy, I don't see why there'd be a problem for both of us to continue our way of living, as long as we keep it secret from our overly conservative parents.

It's perfect. All I have to endure is the wedding and the damn preparations and parties that come with it. Our families are going all out with this, and we – the well-trained puppets that we are - go along with everything they want.

I hate every minute of this bizarre circus, and I hate even more that they want to include us in every single step of the planning process, thus robbing me of valuable time that could be spent elsewhere. Between a pretty girl's legs, for example. I picked up a particularly cute one at the VIP section in a club a few nights ago. A cute brunette with huge eyes and firm tits that she wants me to believe are real, but I can't be fooled. I'm not a fan of fake, but those perky tits drive me insane. I can't wait to see them bouncing up and down again as that little slut rides my thick cock into oblivion.

Alas, I have to waste my Friday evening with this idiotic meeting to discuss the details of our upcoming engagement party in a few weeks. We already discussed the guest list and parts of the catering menu today, both of which took hours to decide because Gloria decided to suddenly have an opinion on these things and engaged in long debates with both of our mothers.

Gloria and I were the first to return to the drawing room to discuss the last matter for today: the musical accompaniment. My mother is a trained actress and attended Juilliard School before she married my father. She feels very close to her alma mater and insisted on hiring one of their students to accompany the engagement party and possibly every event that follows.

My father and both of Gloria's parents were not supportive of the idea, but they filed it under my mother's well-known whimsical traits and decided to let her have this one, if the student managed to convince us with his or her skills.

That's why we're having this ridiculous get-together on a Friday evening. I know Gloria and I share the sentiment of not wanting to be here. She keeps checking her costly watch again and again.

"Where is everybody?" she asks in a nagging voice that drills through my skull.

However, her question is legit. Both of our parents are late, which is very unusual for them.

The double door behind my back squeaks and Gloria lifts her eyes. Her annoyed frown is instantly replaced by a bright smile as she gets up from the sofa she's been sitting on.

I follow her lead and get up myself, fixing my suit in the process, as I turn around to face the door. Gloria's parents enter the room, greeting us with polite nods as they walk in. They're followed by my father and my mother - and her.

The girl who'll rob me of my sanity.

CHAPTER III

Elodie

Mrs. Abrams is a sweetheart. My heart was about to jump out of my chest when I rang the bell at the front door of the Abrams' townhouse. To my surprise, it was Mrs. Abrams herself who opened the door for me, welcoming me in with a big smile. For some reason, I expected a servant to take care of that. Isn't that what super rich people spend their money on?

This family is beyond super rich, though. I knew this before, but I haven't been able to grasp the extent of their wealth until now that I'm stepping into their home. Located right between Park and Lexington avenues, the townhouse boasts a large center entry set in a limestone base and white brick upper stories highlighted by two large, arched windows on the parlor floor. When entering, one steps into a large entrance hall with stairs leading to the upper floors on the left, next to an elevator. An elevator! This is a single family home with five stories *and* its own elevator!

I try not to gawk as Mrs. Abrams introduces me to her husband and another middle-aged couple who turn out to be the bride's parents. All four of them are the epitome of Upper East Side high society when it comes to their looks. The women are both dressed in suit ensembles, accompanied by heavy gold jewelry that - no doubt - costs more than my monthly rent. Maybe even half a year's worth of rent. Their make-up and hairstyle are so similar that one could mistake them for siblings, except for the fact that Mrs. Abrams' hair is a dark auburn color while Mrs. Waldorf is a light blonde. The fathers, both men with graying hair and round bellies, are dressed in tailored suits and sporting clunky watches.

All four of them make me feel horribly under-dressed, even though I'm wearing my most formal dress, a light beige formal-type dress with a lace design that ends just above my knees. I bought it years ago at a second-hand store and have been using it ever since for most of my formal engagements, even performances. It looks pretty worn-out by now, but there's nothing I can do about it, as I live from hand to mouth every single month since I've moved to New York. It's the only formal piece I own, and if this family is to hire me for more than one occasion, I will have to spend some of my earnings to buy another dress so as not to embarrass myself. The same goes for my shoes, an old pair of white ballerinas that used to be chic about a decade ago. Both my dress and my shoes are brand name products, but they were used when I bought them and have suffered through many occasions and performances throughout my time at college.

"So, you're in your final year at Juilliard I hear?" Mrs. Abrams asks in a high-pitched voice as I follow her and the others to the back of the townhouse.

"Yes, I am," I reply, incapable of saying anything other than that, because my head is filled with "Holy shit!" exclamations at every step we take. The entire home is penetrated by light thanks to the insanely high ceilings, open spaces and windows, and the decor is out of this world exquisite and surprisingly tasteful. As the family leads me to the other side of the first floor, I realize that the square footage of this building must be a lot bigger than one would expect from the outside.

"You know, I'm a Juilliard alumnus myself," Mrs. Abrams says, catching my attention.

"Oh, I didn't know that," I reply truthfully.

She smiles at me. "Yes, very few people do. I majored in drama, but I haven't acted in decades."

Mrs. Abrams pauses and lets out a nostalgic sigh. "Sometimes I really miss it."

Before I can come up with a reply, we pass through beautifully adorned french doors, and our short conversation is interrupted by the appearances of what I assume to be the happy couple.

"Miss Hill," Mrs. Abrams says, as we enter the room. "May I introduce you to my son, Kingston, and his beautiful fiancée, Gloria."

She gestures towards the two of them, and I stand awkwardly as they rise from their seats and approach me. Neither of them looks particularly happy to see me. The woman, who is probably about my age but appears to be much older with the way she's styled up, barely manages to smile as she takes my hand, and the groom...

When he shakes my hand, squeezing it a little too hard for my comfort, it feels as if he shoots an electric jolt through my system.

He is devastatingly handsome.

I've tried not to gawk since I entered this home, but now that I lay eyes on him, I can't help but lose control of myself. He's too much, too much of everything. His black hair is cut in a sideswept undercut, gelled to the side with a few strands falling into his handsome face. Just like the fathers, he's wearing a tailored suit in dark gray, but the way his jacket stretches around his arms and chest, it is a reliable telltale of the buff stature hidden beneath. He fixates on me through dark gray eyes, the hint of a smirk appearing on his face, as he welcomes me.

"Pleasure to meet you, Miss Hill," he says. I get weak in the knees as his deep voice radiates through the hall-like sitting room.

Holy shit. How on earth am I supposed to make a good impression with this man around? And he's about to get married, too!

My voice is nothing but a hoarse screech when I try to give him a reply, but no one seems to notice or care.

"Please, let's sit down," Mrs. Abrams says, gesturing towards the seating area where the couple has been waiting for us.

I hesitate for a moment, unsure where to sit, and so I wait for everyone else to take their seats. As it turns out, there is no specific sitting order except for the fact that Mrs. Abrams gestures toward a noble armchair with white cushioning and a wooden frame for me to sit in. The chair is placed next to an array of two sofas and two other armchairs of a similar design, all of them arranged around a white coffee table. I notice that each of the parents sit together on the sofas, while Gloria and Kingston quickly decide on the armchairs, sitting opposite of each other - and closest to me.

I gulp and sincerely hope that no one notices my nervousness. I'm carrying my music sheets with me in a black folder and I place it in my lap, my fingers clasping around it as if I'm holding on for dear life.

"No need to be nervous, Miss Hill," Mrs. Abrams says, casting me a warm smile. "We just want to have a little chat to get to know you a little and exchange some ideas about the event we intend to hire you for."

"Sure," I say.

I can feel his intense dark eyes on me and see him from the corner of my eye. Why is he staring at me like this? When I turn my head to catch his eyes, I expect him to look away, as most people would do when they're caught staring. But he doesn't. Our eyes lock onto each other for a few awkward seconds, before I give in and evade his gaze.

"Tell us a little about yourself," Mr. Waldorf, the bride's father, says. His tone is the complete opposite of Mrs. Abrams. He's firm and serious, not showing even the hint of a smile as he speaks to me.

"Um, about myself?" I ask, unsure what these people need to know about me other than what kind of music I can provide for them. "Well, as for my repertoire, I-"

"No, no," Mrs. Waldorf interrupts. "We'll talk about that later. Tell us a little about *yourself*. Where are you from?"

I regard her with a confused expression. I didn't expect this to be a proper interview and had prepared for playing more than speaking.

"I'm from New York," I say. "Born and raised. Brooklyn."

"That's not New York," Gloria interjects, eyeing her thickly painted finger nails.

"Gloria!" her mother says, casting her a warning look. "Don't be rude."

Gloria rolls her eyes and throws me a disgusted look before she goes back to examining her fingernails, not afraid to show how little she cares about my feelings.

What a bitch.

"Brooklyn, that's... nice," Mrs. Abrams says, sounding a bit helpless. "And your parents, are they also musicians?"

My mother was a drug addict who took off with her lover when I was three years old, that is if I am to believe my father. According to him, she may have died of an overdose not long after leaving us. But I don't know if I can trust his words, considering that he's an alcoholic himself and never forgave my mother for leaving him alone with me. I have no memories of her and never tried to find her. If what little my father told me about her is true, I don't think I'm missing out on anything.

He took care of me as well as he could, but that doesn't say a lot about his parenting skills. I haven't seen him for months, and I only check up on him once in a while to make sure that he's still alive and doing okay. Our interaction is heavily dependent on what kind of woman he is dating at the time. The bitchier they are, the less I hear from him.

"Um, no," I say, hoping that no one presses me on the matter.

"When did you start taking piano lessons?" Mr. Waldorf wants to know.

"Well, I didn't take proper lessons until junior high school," I admit. "But I've played the piano long before that."

My reply is met with awkward silence. I know that most serious musicians started their lessons way younger than that, often even before they started school, but I didn't have that opportunity. We had no money for lessons and no piano at home. All I had was Miss Knight, an elementary teacher who took pity on me and let me play the piano at our school. She even bought me sheet music and taught me a few lessons for free until I graduated. She was also the one who got me started on applying for scholarships to finance my musical education and finally take lessons at the age of fourteen.

"She made it into Juilliard, so she must be good," Mrs. Abrams comes to my rescue. "They only take the best."

"I could play something," I suggest, lifting the folder with my sheets. "Just to give you an idea of my portfolio."

I was told that the family owns a grand piano, as every self-respecting family on the Upper East Side does. Aside from my anxiety to meet the family, I have been looking forward to playing on their piano, as I'm sure it must be a more exquisite instrument than any other I've ever played.

And that assumption doesn't even come close to the truth.

CHAPTER IV

Kingston

I watch as our little piano girl examines our Steinway concert grand piano, her thin fingers caressing the keys, but barely touching them, as if she was afraid she could hurt them. All eyes are on her, observing her peculiar behavior as she fondles the instrument. No one has said a word since we brought her up to the music room, a room that features nothing but the spic and span grand piano surrounded by white walls and a few armchairs lined up against the wall opposite the windows.

"This is a Steinway Concert Grand Model D," the girl gasps without turning around. Her eyes are glued to the piano lid. "It's so... beautiful."

"Isn't it?" my mother agrees, now walking closer to her.

"You know I took a few lessons myself while I was still at Juilliard," she says. "But I never came close to being any good. It's just a hobby for me."

Miss Hill looks at my mother, her eyes wide with curiosity.

"So it does get played?" she asks.

My mother nods. "I toy around with it once in a while. Just to relax, you know. Always playing the same few melodies. It would be a pity if no one would ever use it."

The girl nods. "Yes, it would be!"

"Kingston can play, too," my mother adds, causing all heads to turn in my direction. "He took lessons for a few years while growing up."

I shake my head. It's true that I was forced to take lessons as a child, but it must have been years since I touched a piano.

"Nothing to brag about," I say, trying to divert attention away from me.

My mother smiles at Miss Hill, and I can tell that she's completely in her element. Ever since my brother and I were young children, she's been talking about how much she misses the world of the performing arts. She's always been involved in some kind of fundraising and charity activity to support students of the arts, especially those who - like Miss Hill - don't have the monetary access to lessons. My father doesn't support her love for these activities, but there's very little he can say about it now that her burden as a mother and homemaker has lessened.

"Please," she says, gesturing toward the piano bench. "Play for us."

Miss Hill nods, clasping her black folder as she carefully takes her seat on the bench. She places the folder on the music rack and begins to adjust the bench, while my mother beckons for the rest of us to sit down.

Again, I make sure not to sit next to Gloria. I don't want to deal with her exasperated breaths as she endures Miss Hill's performance. Until just a few minutes ago, I would have been on the same page as her and have shown equally low interest in this.

But that was before *this* girl showed up. This sweet, innocent girl who is the complete opposite of the woman I am to marry. She's raw and pure, incapable of hiding how intimidated she is by this whole situation. Her pale complexion, the chocolate brown hair, and her big green eyes, captured me from the very first moment I saw her.

She's different.

And I like different.

She's also as forbidden as can be, because messing around with her could put this entire charade at risk.

And I fucking *love* forbidden.

She's taken her seat on the bench and now looks up, those big, beautiful eyes widened in question.

"Start with something simple and familiar," my mother answers her silent question. "Something classical that would be a good fit for some mellow background music."

"Debussy maybe?" the girl asks.

"Clair de lune!" my mother completes her suggestion. "That's a good one."

Miss Hill nods.

I watch her face as she places her dainty fingers on the keyboard. It's hard to tell, but I think she lets out a faint sigh as her fingertips touch the keys. I've never seen anyone taken by a simple instrument as much as she is right now. It's hauntingly beautiful to watch.

And sexy as fuck.

It seems she doesn't need her sheets for that one, as she just starts to play right away. She flinches when the first few very soft tunes echo through the room. As the melody speeds up, she closes her eyes and it seems as if she's the one following where the song goes instead of playing it herself. Her brown hair falls over her shoulders when she leans forward during the louder middle path and her lips part as if she was singing along. Her expression is so passionate that I cannot help but wonder if that is what she looks like when climaxing.

I want to make her look that way while she's pinned down beneath my rock-hard body.

My cock needs to knock it the fuck off.

I shift around on my chair, changing my seating position to hide the growing bulge in my crotch.

This is new. You'd think I'm suffering from blue balls, but my encounter with that sexy brunette from the club was not that long ago.

That's not it.

Yet, I've never reacted like this to the mere sight of a woman before. What the hell is happening here?

She doesn't even look that sexy in a traditional sense. Nothing about her screams sex like it does with the vixen from the club. Her dress looks worn out and I know that neither Gloria nor our mothers would ever want to be seen in something like that. There are even a few threads hanging out at the side right below her arm. I bet she didn't notice when she put it on before she came here. Her shoes look equally used and are just as much a telltale sign of her poverty as is the dress.

Her makeup is subtle and I'm sure she stepped it up a notch for today. I'm sure her lips are naked and I'm looking at her natural color, as I imagine them wrapped around my hard cock.

Her play intensifies, and she's long forgotten about our presence in the room. She's lost in the music, her upper body swaying along with the melody and her eyes are still closed, even at the sections I'd imagine are the hardest to play.

Her fingers remain on the last keys as she ends the song and freezes in a bent-over position, while the last note echoes through the room.

Even when my mother starts the applause and we chime in, the girl doesn't look up from the piano. Her eyes remain closed for a few more moments, before she finally opens them, casting a dreamy gaze across the piano lid. She almost looks as if she cannot believe that she was the one who just played that melody.

"Beautiful!" my mother praises, while Gloria barely lifts her eyes from her phone.

Finally, Miss Hill looks at us, a shy smile appearing on her face.

"A very common song, though," Gloria's father interjects. "Do you have anything more out of the ordinary? More complex?"

She looks at him, quiet for a few moments, as she ponders her reply. Just as she opens her mouth to say something, she's interrupted by Gloria's mother.

"Nothing too special, though," she says. "There's no need to get too esoteric, we still want people to recognize the music as their own. We'd like to play a few of their favorites."

She casts her husband a warning look and he shrugs.

"Yes, absolutely," Miss Hill says. "I have a few pieces in mind that are perfect for a romantic musical accompaniment, such as the 2nd movement of Beethoven's Pathetique or some of Chopin's more docile salon pieces."

"Chopin!" my mother sighs. "Oh, he is one of my favorites!"

The girl's face lights up.

"Mine, too," she says. "Personally, I'd suggest some of the Nocturnes - Opus 9 in e-flat major for example - or his preludes in F sharp major, Ab major and maybe even the Db major. Next to his waltzes, which could also be played to-"

"I think we get the idea, Miss Hill," my father interrupts her. "There's no need to get too much into the detail. I think Kingston and Gloria should have a say in this, as well."

He throws expectant looks first at me, then at Gloria, who manages just in time to fake interest in the whole conversation.

"What do you think?" my father asks. "Is there anything in particular you wish to hear?"

I gesture toward Gloria, implying that she should be the first to speak, but she just shrugs her shoulders.

"Classical sounds good, I guess," she says.

"I could also play John Williams variations or Phillip Glass," Miss Hill says, trying to catch Gloria's attention. "To add a modern touch to the repertoire."

Gloria furls her eyebrows. "Who?"

"Movie composers," I enlighten her. "Especially Glass, who has written a lot of piano pieces."

From the corner of my eyes, I can see Miss Hill nodding.

"I don't think we want to go in that direction," my mother interjects, speaking as if we just suggested turning the engagement party into an alternative rock concert. "Just show us a few more of your classical pieces."

Miss Hill nods quietly and closes her eyes to devote herself to another song.

CHAPTER V

Elodie

I t's like they're not even here. While I play on this beautiful piano - a freaking Steinway Model D concert grand piano - I forget everything and everyone else around me. I forget where I am, who's watching me, and what this whole performance is about.

It doesn't feel like a performance, or like I have to prove myself right now. Once I start playing, nothing else matters. It's just me and one of the greatest pianos I have every played on. The sound is out of this world, and I feel as if I'm bathing in the music.

The only thing I cannot block out are his eyes on me. A normal person would let their gaze travel, maybe even close their eyes to suspend the one sense that is utterly redundant, to enjoy a good piece of music.

But he doesn't.

He's staring at me nonstop, and it's the only thing that makes it hard for me to get completely lost in the music, as I usually would.

Yet, I can barely hide my disappointment when Mr. Abrams announces that they have heard enough for today. The family decides that I should create a playlist for the evening that is long enough to fill about three hours. Mrs. Abrams is the only one who adds suggestions to the list, which leaves me pretty much on my own.

"So, you want me to play?" I ask, as everybody is getting ready to leave the room and escort me outside.

Mrs. Abrams turns to me, tilting her head to the side and smiling, as if I'd just asked a very stupid question.

"But of course, dear," she says. "Why would we not?"

I feel a wave of relief traveling down my spine. Even though I had the bliss of getting lost in the music for the few minutes while I was playing, I sort of took this meeting to be an audition. But Mrs. Abrams is making it sound as if they'd been sure of hiring me even before I showed up today.

"I... er, I just wanted to make sure," I stutter.

She smiles and places her hand on my shoulder.

"Your play was wonderful," she says. "And we're looking forward to having you perform at the engagement party in two months."

Two months. That's still so far away. On one hand, it leaves me with a lot of time to prepare, but it also means that I won't be seeing any money until shortly before my graduation.

Everybody but Mrs. Abrams and her sinfully handsome son has already excused themselves and left the room. As Mrs.

Abrams escorts me down the stairs, her son walks closely behind us, looming over us with his tall stature as she raves about her time at Juilliard. It's obvious that she still feels very connected to our school, even though her time as a student was such a long time ago.

"If you don't mind," she says, as we reach the entrance door, "we will have to meet again at least twice before the actual event. Once in about a week to go over the play list for the evening, and another time to further discuss the evening's schedule. We might have little addresses and such, and the music should be planned accordingly."

She stops speaking and turns toward her son, who - for whatever reason - is standing right next to us, locking me down with his intense stare and making my insides vibrate with a dangerous desire due to his proximity. I can even breathe in his intoxicating smell.

How can he not be aware of his effect on women? Why is he still here? Shouldn't he have left with his fiancée?

"Also, Gloria and Kingston might wish to add a little dance," she says, tilting her head again. "A newly engaged waltz maybe?"

He finally takes his eyes off of me and regards his mother with a polite but distant smile.

"We'll see," he says to her, before turning back to me. "How are you getting home, Miss Hill?"

"Oh, I'll just take the subway, it's not far," I hurry to say.

"Nonsense," he says. "Let me give you a ride home. You live on campus, I assume?"

I hastily shake my head.

"It's really not far, I can just-"

"Oh, don't be shy," his mother says. "Let my son be a gentleman and make sure you get home safely. A young lady shouldn't be out by herself in the dark in Manhattan."

What?!

I'm inclined to tell her how ridiculous that sounds to me. She and I live in completely different worlds, and mine certainly doesn't provide personal drivers or even the possibility to call for a cab whenever needed.

"I was about to drive downtown anyway," he says. "I can make a little detour to Juilliard."

Oh, please God no. The thought of being alone with him kills me.

"Really, it's not-"

But my protest is silenced once again by Mrs. Abrams, who thanks her son for making the offer and opens the door to let us out. We say our goodbyes and I follow him outside, my legs shaking.

It's become cold outside, and I just now realize that I forgot to bring a cardigan with me to wear over my thin dress. If it wasn't for him looking and acting the way he does, I would actually be thankful for the ride.

"This is really not necessary," I repeat, while following him around the house where he heads toward a black sports car.

"If you say that one more time, I'm going to drop you off in the middle of the Bronx," he says, as he opens the door for me.

I flush as I squeeze past him and my crummy dress skims the expensive fabric of his attire. The contrast between us is so vast, it makes me feel incredibly uncomfortable.

He closes the door behind me and runs around the car to take his seat on the driver's side. The awkward flutter I felt while just standing next to him is nothing compared to the way I feel now that we're sitting right next to each other, alone, in a confined space. He starts the engine and drives out on to the street, and I realize that I cannot even remember the last time I've sat in a car, let alone a car that was driving through Manhattan.

"You really liked that piano, didn't you," he says, casting me a quick look from the side.

"It's a beautiful instrument," I say. "I barely get to play on a grand piano like that. Even for performance, they barely provide a Model D. They are expensive and rare!"

He chuckles. "I guess so. I have to agree I've never spent much thought on it."

Of course, he hasn't, and I feel like an idiot for getting so excited about something that means nothing to him. He must think I'm such a nerd.

"You will probably play on the same model during our engagement party," he says. "Don't you think it would make sense for you to practice on ours once in a while until then?"

I look at him, my eyes wide with surprise and confusion. "What?"

"I'm sure it could be arranged," he says, glancing over at me so that our eyes meet for a second.

Damn, he's handsome. How can a man be so beautiful? Is it the money, his wealth? Am I really that superficial?

No, he's just that good looking, and he would be even if he was wearing a garbage bag.

"That's not necessary," I repeat my mantra from earlier. "We have plenty of pianos at Juilliard and I-"

"I think it would be better if you practiced on ours, in our home," he says. "You wouldn't disturb anyone. It's just my parents who are still living there, and they aren't home that much. Besides, it's a big house and the piano hardly gets used. My mother was kind of exaggerating when she said she'd play once in a while. She does it like twice a year, as far as I know."

My heart sinks at the thought of that. Such a beautiful instrument, and no one playing on it. If I had a Model D in my home, I don't think I could ever stop playing.

Also, if I had a home like that, I would make sure to spend as much time as possible there. Rich people really don't appreciate what they have.

"I... really don't want to impose," I whisper, clutching my sheets.

The thought of being able to play on this beautiful piano on a regular basis for the next few weeks is almost too good to be true, even if it means having to step inside a world that makes me feel incredibly uncomfortable about myself. But I know none of that will matter once I start playing...

"You're not imposing," he insists. "I'm sure my mother agrees that this is a good idea, and my father really doesn't get much say anyway. They'd be glad to let you practice in their home. I'll speak to them."

A heavy lump in my throat prevents me from speaking, or even reacting to what he said. The prospect is too alluring. It flatters and confuses me that he would make this generous suggestion.

"I will need your phone number," he adds, and my heart jumps.

"Why?"

He laughs. "Because I need a way to contact you to let you know when you can use the piano. We might have to set up a schedule."

"I'm sure your parents have it."

"Just to be safe, give it to me, as well," he insists, nodding toward the glove compartment. "There's a pen and notebook in there. Write it down."

My eyes wander back and forth between him and the glove compartment. This feels weird and wrong. Why do I feel like he's hitting on me? He's engaged! Am I really that dazed by how handsome he is?

Still, I do as he tells me and leave my phone number, just for him.

CHAPTER VI

Kingston

"And did you see her *dress*?" Gloria asks in that shrill and obnoxious voice of hers. "It was pretty much falling apart!"

She's sitting across the table from me, as we're enduring another family tea time during which we have to pretend to be a couple who cares enough for each other to not mind getting married.

Even our parents know that it's not love that makes us take this big step, but they don't care. It's not what they need from us. They just need us to be content with the situation. Content, well-behaved and settled, ready to provide the much anticipated grandchildren. I still don't know how we'll pull off that part, considering we can barely stand to be in the same room, let alone touch each other. I guess we will cross that bridge when we get there.

"Oh, the dress," Mrs. Waldorf chimes in. "How embarrassing! To show up at our house looking like a beggar. I could hardly look at it."

I roll my eyes, and I'm glad to see that my parents have the decency not to join Gloria and her mother in their hateful gossip. However, they also shy away from putting these women in their place.

"She will have to find something more suitable to wear," my father agrees. "But I have no issue with her performance. I think she'll do a good job, and she's very willing to go along with our wishes."

"For a very cheap price," my mother adds, as if anyone cared about the amount of money that's thrown at this whole endeavor. "I think hiring a Juilliard student will set a great precedence to put eyes on our families' efforts to support the performing arts. A prestigious school like Juilliard will always appreciate goodwill from an Upper East Side family and word of it will get around."

"It will do our reputation good," Mr. Waldorf agrees. "But only if this girl doesn't embarrass us."

"She won't," I say, surprised at my own voice.

All eyes are turning to me. Their surprise is more due to the fact that I speak at all, as I usually keep rather quiet during these bothersome get-togethers.

"However, I'd suggest that her play itself is more important than what dress she's wearing," I add.

"Yes," my mother says, knowing where I'm going with this, as I've already discussed the issue with her in private.

"Kingston suggested that she be allowed to use our grand piano for practice, so she can get accustomed to the feel and sound of it," she enlightens the others, and especially my father, who hasn't heard the idea before.

"And I think that's a great idea," my mother continues. "Provided this is all right with you, dear?"

She turns to my father, who just shrugs.

"As long as she's not doing it in the middle of the night and there's someone here to supervise her while she's here," he says. He raises an eyebrow as he looks at my mother. "You know. In case she gets a little too curious or... too fond of our possessions."

"Are you suggesting she'd steal from us?" I ask, disgusted.

My father shrugs. "You never know. Better to be safe than sorry."

"That's right," Gloria says. "You never know with these kinds of girls. She looks desperately poor and like she could be someone to do such a thing."

I take in a deep breath, trying to contain my anger at their disgusting assumptions, but before I can say anything to them, my mother speaks up instead.

"It's not nice to make such assumptions about strangers," she says. "But I agree that it wouldn't be wise to leave her here by herself. I'll try to be home, and if that's not possible, we can still ask her to come when our maid, Wally is here."

Or me, I think to myself.

I'm not suggesting it out loud, as I don't want to draw too much attention on the idea of myself and Elodie alone in the house. I have to fake an utter disinterest in her, and also have to watch myself when it comes to defending her in front of my family. But of course, this is all I can think of. Me and her. Alone.

The ride in my car was too short and too immediate to make any kind of move. It was too soon to tell how she'd react. I just used the very few minutes we had with each other to feel her out. I needed to know if she was responsive to me. Her expressions, the way she spoke and behaved in my presence were enough for me to know if she'd respond, and how.

And there was a response. A very strong response. She shifted in her seat, kept playing with her delicate fingers in her lap, and barely managed to maintain eye contact with me for more than a second. I make her feel something without even touching her. It's beautiful to watch, and insanely addictive.

I didn't tell anyone that she obediently scribbled down her phone number for me, and when I told my mother about the idea of her practicing on our grand piano, I suggested that she arrange for that to happen. I didn't ask Elodie to give me her phone number so I could contact her regarding this, I only asked her to see if she'd give it to me, if she'd be a good girl and do as I ask her to.

And she did.

CHAPTER VII

Elodie

Once again, I find myself standing in front of the Abrams family's extravagant townhouse. It has only been a few days since our first meeting, but Mrs. Abrams was quick to contact me about the possibility of practicing in her house, just as Kingston had suggested. Coming up with a schedule that suited both of us wasn't easy, as I'm busy with classes and my part time job, and she had wanted to make sure there was someone around the house every time I stop by. I don't know what she does that keeps her so busy since she doesn't have – or need – a regular full-time job, but she confessed that she was rarely home so I'd most likely be greeted by one of their personal servants every time I come by.

It was a relief to hear that Kingston Abrams doesn't live here, so I shouldn't have to worry about him showing up. As far as I know, no one is home this afternoon, so I'm not surprised when a middle-aged woman with an unfamiliar face opens the door for me.

"You must be Elodie," she says, giving me a bright smile. "My name is Wally."

That's an unusual name for a woman, but it's one that suits her. Her round cheeks and obvious warm heart reminds me of a young grandma. It's a refreshing change from the rather cold and artificial demeanor of the Waldorf and Abrams women who greeted me the last time.

"Yes. It's so nice to meet you," I say, following her gesture motioning me to come inside. "I hope I'm not causing you any trouble..."

"Oh, dear, not at all," Wally says, waving me off. "I'm glad to have some musical company while I'm cleaning. I already finished the floor with the musical room to make sure I wouldn't disturb you."

"Thank you," I say, casting her a grateful smile.

"Stay and play as long as you wish," she adds. "The Abrams have a dinner commitment for tonight, so they won't be home for several hours."

I'm glad to hear this, as I'm not exactly dressed to impress today so wouldn't mind avoiding a meeting with the home owners. I'm wearing black skinny jeans and a simple light baby blue blouse that I bought at a thrift store not too long ago. I consider the outfit to be tasteful and attractive, but it obviously doesn't compare to the styles typically worn around this house.

Wally leads me up to the music room and then excuses herself, letting me know that she'll be on one of the other floors doing her job while I practice. It seems odd to me that it's just the two of us alone in a house that's not home to either one of us, and none of the owners are here.

She closes the door after she's left, leaving me alone. It's just me and the grand piano. I take in the view of the beautiful instrument before I take my seat on the bench and get ready to play. The piano really does have a different feel to it than the one I usually practice on, so Kingston's idea of letting me practice on this once ahead of the event was actually a good one.

I still wonder to myself why he suggested it, though.

As I begin to warm up by playing a few scales, my thoughts travel back to him. The most handsome man I've ever met, the richest, the sexiest – and he's engaged. But why is he so nice to me? And why did he look at me like that? If I didn't know any better, I would have sworn that he was flirting with me.

I smile and shake my head. I'm just being silly.

Of course he wasn't flirting. Even if he wasn't engaged, he's so far out of my league that the thought of him showing even the slightest interest in me is outright ridiculous.

Maybe he's just a nice guy. He must have been raised to be a gentleman, after all. It could be normal for him to escort a woman home to make sure she gets there safely.

Time flies by as I work my way through a few pieces that I'm quite familiar with. I've come up with a preliminary play list for the evening, but I'm determined to add a few more complex pieces even though my confidence in them is not as high. Before I tackle that challenge, though, I decide to give myself a break to play something just for myself. After all, no one said I'm not allowed to enjoy myself a little while I'm here.

I continue with one of Chopin's Nocturnes. Its sad and heavy tones may not be suitable for an engagement celebration, but I love the meditative and quiet character of it. If I ever was to get married, I would love to hear all 21 of Chopin's nocturnal pieces on that special day.

I'm so lost in the music that I don't notice the door to my right – and him. I don't know how long he's been there, but when our eyes meet, it sends a sudden wave of shock through my system. The realization that he's standing right next to the door, watching me, leaning against the wall with his arms folded in front of his strong chest, completely throws off my focus. I stop in the middle of the last part of the song, a return to the cantabile melody of the piece after an energetic middle part.

He laughs as I gasp for air, trying to regain my composure.

"I'm sorry," Kingston Abrams says, casting me the most charming smile. "I didn't want to startle the artist."

He's not wearing a suit today, but instead he's sporting a more casual outfit. However, he looks just as handsome and perfect in a soft cashmere sweater and black pants as he did in the tailored suit a few days ago.

"No, it's okay," I say. "Is it time for me to leave?"

I'm already in the process of gathering up my sheets, but he shakes his head and steps closer to the piano.

"No, please," he says gesturing towards the grand piano. "Stay as long as you wish, my parents will be out until late. You're not bothering anyone."

"Oh... okay," I mumble, withdrawing my hands from the sheets.

Why is he here then?

"I just wanted to say 'Hi' and see if everything is going okay for you up here," he answers my unspoken question.

He's standing right next to the piano now, towering over me with his impressive stature. It's awkward to talk to him when he's standing in this way, and I feel a strong urge to get up from the bench to win some height on him, but I reckon he'll be leaving the room shortly so I don't bother to move.

"Everything is fine," I say. "Thank you again for making this possible. I love this piano. It has such a different feel than the ones I'm used to."

He smiles at me. "I liked the song you were just playing before I interrupted you."

"Oh, that... I... it might not be suitable for the event, I just –"

"Calm down," he says, raising his hand in a reassuring manner. "You're not on trial here. Play whatever feels right. I really don't care if it's among the pieces that make it onto the list."

I chuckle. "You should care. It's *your* engagement party, after all."

I bite my tongue. Why on earth did I say that? After he's been so nice to me, I actually have the nerve to lecture him?

"Yeah," he says absentmindedly. "I guess it is."

He doesn't look happy as he says it. His gaze wanders off, scanning the room seemingly lost in thought.

"Is there a song you'd like for me to play that night?" I ask him. "So far your mother is the only one who has offered any input, so I'm pretty much working with my own ideas."

He shakes his head. "No. My wishes don't count in this."

I look up at him quizzically, trying to read his expression. He must know that I'm looking at him, but he chooses to ignore it and evade my eyes by looking out the window on the other side of the vast room.

"Or your fiancée," I say. "Gloria. Does she have any wishes?"

He laughs as if the idea itself is ridiculous.

"Believe me, she doesn't care at all," he says, now turning to reciprocate my look. "Things in this family don't follow the rules of Disney or a cheesy romance flick."

I furl my eyebrows and nervously play with my unoccupied fingers as I try to figure out what he's trying to say.

"What do you mean?" I daringly ask.

He clears his throat and leans down towards me, supporting himself on the piano lid. His face is scarily close to mine now, and I instinctively move away to create some distance between us. I don't do it because his presence is uncomfortable; I do it because I must.

"What I mean is that things are not always as apparent as they seem," he explains.

What the hell does *that* mean?

His words confuse me. And his proximity is almost too much for me to handle. There's an unspoken tension between us, something that's pulling me toward him while pushing me away at the same time.

It must be his handsome looks. His perfectly edgy face with that rugged touch that makes a man a man. That and the fact that I can see his arm muscles stretching the thin fabric of his exquisite cashmere sweater over his biceps as he supports himself on the piano right next to me.

He's so incredibly attractive. This man screams sex.

"I... I don't know what that means," I stutter, shifting on the bench in an attempt to move away from him.

But he doesn't let me.

I freeze when I feel his strong hand on my shoulder, keeping me in place with just a hint of force. His touch is electric, warm, terrifying.

I never knew that women could have blue balls, too, because I don't think I've ever been this desperate for a man's touch.

That can't be it, can it? He's just freakishly handsome, charming, masculine, rich. He's the embodiment of almost every woman's dream, and the worst thing is that he knows it. Under this gentlemanly exterior could be a ruthless player. God knows he could get any woman he wants. If there's a man who fits that description, it's him. He's playing with me, but I hate to be a puppet in his sick little game.

I can't help but feel sorry for Gloria – and I can hear Wally rummaging around downstairs. It's making me all the more uncomfortable.

I calmly reach up to his hand on my shoulder and move it away. He lets it happen without a fight and straightens up, creating the much needed distance between us. I feel relieved and disappointed at the same time.

"I think you do know what that means," he says.

Our eyes meet, and for a few very awkward and very intense moments, we just stare at each other as we're having a conversation without speaking.

"Would you do me a favor?" he asks, breaking the tense silence between us.

I tilt my head to the side, afraid of what he might ask of me. "Yes?"

"Play that song again," he says. "The song you were playing before you noticed me. I'd like to hear it again."

"It's really not appropriate for the event –"

"I don't care," he interrupts me. "This is just for me."

He walks away from the piano and takes a seat in one of the chairs lined up against the wall next to the door. My eyes follow him as he crosses his legs and casts me an expectant look.

"I don't give private concerts," I try to joke, displaying a sass that's not typically part of my character.

"There's a first time for everything," he says, jutting his chin forward. "Play."

So I do as I'm told.

CHAPTER VIII

Kingston

W hat a good girl she is. I watch as she turns her attention back to the keys in front of her, lowering her eyes and taking in a deep breath before she begins playing the soft tunes marking the beginning of what I know to be one of Chopin's best Nocturnes. If I'm not mistaken, it's from his Opus posthumous.

I never cared much for classical music, at least not as much as I was expected to. But my mother always stood on musical education and made sure that both my younger brother and I obtained at least a basic knowledge if not an appreciation for classical music from different eras. Even though we were forced to take piano lessons as children, neither of us ever developed a passion for it.

Actually we sucked. It was a frustrating endeavor for everyone involved, including my mother and our teachers.

But it left me with enough of an understanding to appreciate Elodie's talent. I've never heard anything like the sounds she's producing right now echoing through the halls of my family's home. We've had this grand piano forever, and I remember every one of the God awful hours I spent in this room as a child, waiting for time to pass so I could go back to doing anything besides practicing the piano.

I don't understand the joy in playing the piano, but it's evident all over Elodie's face. My eyes don't leave her for a second while she's playing, but she doesn't seem to be fazed by it at all. It's like she doesn't even notice that I'm here. She's too lost in her playing, waving and moving with her eyes closed, her lips partly opened as she experiences the sensation of the music she's creating.

I didn't lie when I said that I liked the song. Chopin and his sinister Nocturnes are one of the very few things I still remember from my forced musical education, and I only remember them because I liked them.

But Elodie's appreciation for them takes it to a whole other level. Her passion is palpable and contagious. Her slim shoulders waltz up and down, causing the light fabric of her blue blouse to wrinkle around her perky breasts. She left three buttons unbuttoned, something that would have been seductive had she any cleavage to show. This way, all I can see is her collarbone and the narrow trail that leads down between her boobs.

If seeing her play like this is erotic, I can't even imagine what it would do to me to see her on this bench completely naked. Or partly naked. Maybe even tied up.

I search for her feet, the right one working the piano pedal while the left one rests tucked away under the bench. She wouldn't be able to play properly if I tied her ankles to the bench, but I'd happily make that sacrifice if I got to see her like that, moving like she is now, closing her eyes, parting her lips, her body weaving with the melody while she's restrained and tied to the bench.

Maybe a little vibrator forced against her clit...

Fuck, she drives me insane.

I shift on the chair, repositioning my legs and trying to hide the bulge protruding in my lap.

I have to have her. I don't care how risky it is, I don't care if I have to share my dirty little secret with her. She's a good girl. She already withdrew from me once, and I can practically see the red stop sign appearing in front of her eyes every time she lets herself embark on the idea of acting on our forbidden attraction.

Yet, she likes to obey. She unconsciously expresses an evident satisfaction when she follows my wishes.

I know she's feeling it, too. I can see it in the way she looks at me, the way her voice changes when she talks, the way her hands always nervously search for something to do every time I talk to her.

Of course, she wants this, too. For fuck's sake, look at me. I know what I am and how I look. I know about the effect I have on women; I'm not fucking stupid.

However, neither is she. She's not as easy and superficial as the girls I usually pursue. She may even think that she's not the kind of girl for a no strings-attached adventure with a guy like me. She may even have a boyfriend. Of course, that wouldn't stop me, but it would make going after her so much harder.

In any case, I can't let her think that I'm cheating on my beloved soon-to-be wife. She certainly doesn't want to be *that* girl. So, I know what's going to have to be my first step.

Telling her the ugly truth about my engagement, or at least parts of it.

The song ends and she basks in the last few notes, not yet ready to look up at me. It feels wrong to applaud, so I give her a few moments before I get up and walk back over to the piano.

She lifts her head and her eyes meet mine when I come to a halt next to the piano lid. She's smiling, but I know that it's not a smile meant for me, but for the man who wrote this piece she loves so much.

"Very nice," I praise her. "Brilliant song, excellently played."

"It's a Nocturne from the –"

"Opus posthumous," I finish her sentence. "Yes, I know. I'm familiar with it."

Her eyes light up. "Oh, so you're a fan of Chopin?"

I give her a smirk and shake my head.

"I wouldn't call it that," I say. "But I've heard his Nocturnes a few times, and I agree that this one is probably the best."

She nods, lowering her shoulders in a display of slight disappointment.

Sorry girl, I'm not a classical music nerd as much as you are.

She reaches over to the other side of the piano lid, right next to her music sheets, and grabs her phone to take a quick glance at it.

"Oh my God, I've been here for more than two hours!" she exclaims. "I really should be going."

"Do you have anywhere to be?" I ask her.

She looks up at me, obvious fright in her eyes. She's scared that I'm going to offer to drive her home again. So fucking cute.

"No, not really, I just..." she stutters. "I mean, I'd be practicing at this time anyway, it's one of the few afternoons and evening that I have off."

"Off?" I ask. "From school?"

She huffs, shaking her head with a smile that seems to belittle me, as if I should know better.

"Work," she says. "I have a part time job at the University's coffee shop."

Of course she does. And I actually did reveal a certain degree of ignorance by not automatically assuming she's not privileged enough to be able to put all her focus on her studies.

"So, that's what you do with a free afternoon," I say, nodding toward the sheet music. "You practice?"

She shrugs. "Yes. I enjoy it, and there's no such thing as too much practice."

"I think there is," I tell her. "There's a reason why there's so much talk about work-life-balance. People get fucked up when they overdo it. You need some time to rest, to refresh and clear that pretty head of yours."

She blushes and glances at me, only to evade my eyes a second later by staring down at the keys in front of her. So fucking alluring.

"I'm okay," she says, her voice so low that I can barely hear her. "I wouldn't even know what else to do."

So, she's going to ignore that I just called her pretty. She's not calling me out on it, and I kind of expected that. But she's not unfazed by it.

"Want me to give you some ideas?" I ask, leaning on the rim of the piano.

She takes in a deep breath and shakes her head.

"I really should be going," she repeats.

She gets up from the bench and hastily starts gathering up her sheets of music.

Fuck, this is one scared lamb.

"What are you afraid of?" I ask her, locking her in place with my intense gaze.

Elodie pauses and turns to me. She's wearing her chocolate brown hair down today and it falls over her shoulders in perfectly calm waves, framing her pale face and her naturally red lips, giving her the appearance of a real-life Snow White. She bites her lower lip and furls her eyebrows just the slightest bit.

"I have nothing to be afraid of," she says eventually. "Right?"

Oh, she couldn't be more wrong.

CHAPTER IX

Elodie

I have no idea what his deal is. Why is he still here? Why did he show up in the first place? What is this supposed to be? Is he making fun of me? How does that add up with the charm he showed me on the day we first met?

Our eyes are locked on each other, and I feel as if he just challenged me to a dare, which is ridiculous.

"If you think you have nothing to be afraid of," he says, "then why are you being so defensive and withdrawn?"

I frown at him. He must be kidding.

"Why are you here?" I finally dare to ask. "You don't live here. Why are you not home with your fiancée?"

"We don't live together," he says. "At least not yet."

That strikes me as odd. Are these families really that old-fashioned? Are they not allowed to live together until they tie the knot? I find that hard to believe.

"I have my own place," he continues. "A very nice penthouse close to the East River. Beautiful views."

He winks at me. "You should come with me and check it out."

Is he serious? I force a laugh and cross my arms protectively in front of my chest.

"What are you suggesting?" I ask, now challenging him. At least that's my intention.

He shrugs, acting as if his flirting with me was the most normal thing on the planet, when it's so clearly not. It's outrageous and wrong on so many levels.

"We both have some free time with nothing to do, and I firmly believe you need to learn to relax and do something better with your time off than practicing," he says. "I see no harm in us having a drink together on my rooftop. Or a little barbeque if you're hungry."

"What? Why?" I ask.

"Why not?" he retorts, slowly driving me mad.

Because you're about to get married? Because even if you weren't, you're way out of my league? Because the last time I did something stupid like this in my free time, it turned out to be a bad mistake? Because you're clearly making fun of me?

"I'm hired to provide music for your engagement party," I remind him. "What makes you think that your invitation is okay?"

He chuckles.

"You're naughtier than you look," he says, causing my cheeks and ears to burn.

Our eyes meet again, and I can see mischief dancing in the dark gray depths of his. He's not as close to me as he was before, but I can still feel his proximity as if he was wrapped snuggly all around me. I can feel his warmth, sense his masculine smell, and I fight the allure of his presence. The way he looks at me reveals that I'm not the one with the ulterior motives, he is.

"All I'm suggesting is for you to have a drink at my place, and maybe a bite to eat," he says. "My treat. As a thank you for your efforts to make my family's party a success."

"Your engagement," I repeat. "What would Gloria think if she knew you're inviting random women to your place for drinks?"

He shrugs again.

"I can assure you, she wouldn't care," he says. "I'm quite positive that she's not alone herself tonight."

My eyes widen. What kind of messed up relationship are these two having? Is it one of those open relationship deals? Polygamy?

Either way, I want nothing to do with it.

"Look," I say. "I don't know what it is that you two are doing, but I want no part of it. I really have to go home."

"You don't have to go home," he insists. "You just said you have nothing to do. You are just scared."

I huff. "Scared? Of what?"

He casts me a confident smirk. "Me."

We stare at each other again, our eyes smoldering, for what feels like an eternity, and I feel trapped. I'm still holding on to my sheet music, as if it could protect me from him and his charming yet confusing propositions.

After the disaster with Benjamin, I swore to myself that I would not get involved with anything messy again. Fooling around with a man who has hired me to play at his engagement party, my first real client outside the Juilliard school environment, a man from a powerful family, a family that could possibly decide about my future as a solo pianist – that would be the epitome of messy.

I won't be that stupid.

"I'm not scared of you," I insist. "But what you're suggesting is making me very uncomfortable."

He furls his eyebrows as if he seems to understand.

"Fine," he says. "Do whatever you deem right."

He straightens up, glaring at me. For a few seconds, I can't help but wonder if this was a test? Did he come on to me like this to see whether I'm a decent woman who can focus on her job instead of being seduced by the most attractive man on earth?

If so, I'd say I passed.

He doesn't give me that impression, though. If anything, he looks like a man who has just been turned down, a man who's not used to being turned down.

He shoves his hands into his pants pockets and retreats.

"Stay as long as you wish," he says. "No one will bother you."

And with that, he turns around and leaves the room, closing the door with a loud bang behind himself.

I remain standing in front of the piano, as if I've just been turned into a pillar of salt, still clutching my music sheets against my chest.

CHAPTER X

Kingston

I knew she'd be a challenge, but I didn't expect her to be that reluctant, that careful.

It was stupid of me to forget that I'm not the only one who'd be risking a lot with this. She has a job to lose, and a reputation to protect. Being hired by my family means more to her than just providing music for that one silly event, or two or three, if we decided to hire her for the rehearsal dinner and the wedding itself.

This is a tough one.

Still, I don't know what it is with her. It seems like I'm losing all the power I usually hold over women. She's intimidated by me and she's attracted to me, but she doesn't lose her mind over me.

Then again, she's not some drunk bimbo at a night club, and I don't have an easy job of it. It's been a while since I've put my assets to work during daylight. The last time was with an intern at my father's company, a girl very much like her. An innocent plain Jane with brown hair and big, unsuspecting eyes. She was afraid about losing her internship when I first approached her, but I managed to get her to trust me, at least in that regard. I don't want to threaten these girls' careers, but I also don't want to end up with them hanging onto my arm for the rest of my life. Sadly, the little intern didn't take that last part into account and left her internship with good references and a broken heart.

I didn't care. It was stupid of her to believe otherwise, and I never said anything that could've made her think that we were meant to have more than a naughty fling.

She was good, though. Delicious. Breaking in girls like her is so much fun because the more they hide and suppress their inner whore on a daily basis, the wilder they get once you peel away that side of them.

That intern chick was good, but I can't even remember her name. Three times, that's it. That's how long it takes before I get bored with them.

It won't be any different with Elodie, but I need to make those three times happen because I know she won't leave my head until I do. Plus, I've never been rejected. Never.

I pace about in my parents' kitchen, contemplating my options. She'll come downstairs any moment now, and I don't want to let her leave just like that. I'll offer to drive her back to campus again, hoping that it'll give me another opportunity.

She'll most likely say no, and I will insist, and we will go from there...

Just as I've made up my mind, I hear music coming from upstairs. She's playing the piano again.

Just a few minutes ago, she was desperate to leave the house, and now that I've left her alone, she just continues to practice?

I walk out into the entrance hall next to the stairs leading to the upper floors and listen to her play. I've been standing there for less than a minute when Wally, our housemaid, shows up. She walks down the stairs with an apologetic expression on her face.

"I'm done for today," she says, as she reaches the first floor and comes to a halt next to me. "I have to go home, my kids need dinner, but I've been told not to leave her in here by herself."

Her gaze turns up the stairs.

"It's so beautiful, isn't it," she adds. "I don't have the heart to tell her to stop."

"It's okay," I say, sensing an opportunity. "I'll stick around and make sure she doesn't rob us blind."

Good old Wally looks at me with eyebrows arched in indignation. "Oh, I don't think she would –"

"Me neither," I assure her. "It's just a precaution my parents are taking. You're free to go, I'll take care of this."

She gives me a warm smile, and tilts her head to the side. "Thank you, Kingston. That is very sweet of you."

It's anything but sweet, but Wally doesn't need to know that.

She leaves, and I'm alone in the house with Elodie, who's still playing her music upstairs. As long as she's playing, I'll know where she is, and I also know that it wouldn't do me any good to go up there and make another move on her.

Instead, I decide to stay downstairs and out of her sight. There's a little sitting area next to the entrance hall. No one ever sits there, and it's usually used for guests who are told to wait when my parents aren't ready to receive them yet.

I sit down in a ridiculous-looking love seat that only a woman with my mother's taste would acquire. The old-fashioned frame and the beige-colored cushions give this piece of furniture the feel of a long gone time. The entire room emits this antiquated feel, and I can't say I care for it. I took great care to make sure that my own home doesn't reflect my parents' taste at all. My penthouse is sleek and modern with steel colors and – as my mother put it – an atmosphere that can only be described as cold as a man's heart. I know she didn't mean anything good by it, but I thanked her for the compliment.

I feel like an idiot sitting here. As if I was a dog waiting for its owner. Men tend to make fools of themselves when they are in pursuit of a woman, but I never saw myself as that pathetic. They usually fall to their knees as soon as I give them any kind of attention, and I'm not used to working this hard for a good fuck. Some would say I'm wasting my time because things could be so much easier if I just went out throwing money around left and right on champagne and chicks in the VIP section, and just take home the one that fancies me the most.

I know I could easily do that, and that's what makes it so boring to me.

When Elodie's music stops for longer than usual, my heart rate spikes up. I get up from my seat and smooth down my clothes like a fucking idiot. As if she'd care about the wrinkles in my sweater.

I hear the door open on the second floor, and I let a few more moments pass before I walk back into the entrance hall, getting there just as she comes down the stairs carrying the bag with her music sheets pressed against her side like a shield. Her eyes widen in surprise when she sees me.

"You're still here," she says, stating the obvious.

"So are you," I say.

She slowly continues making her way downstairs until she's standing right in front of me, holding on to her bag even tighter than before.

"Where's Wally? I'd like to say goodbye," she says.

"I sent her home," I tell her. "She was done with her work and has kids to take care of at home."

"Oh," Elodie says. "Okay..."

She clears her throat and eyes the door. "Well, I'm gonna g-"

"Scared I might ask to take you home again?" I want to know.

She furls her eyebrows. "What is it with you and wanting to see me scared?"

"That's not wishful thinking," I insist. "That's the simple truth. You are scared."

She huffs and shakes her head.

"Well, were you going to make that offer?" she asks, now looking at me with a stern face. It's incredibly endearing.

"No," I say, following a sudden hunch. I'm going to try a different approach.

"Because I don't want you to go home," I add.

She's startled. "Why... not?"

I step closer to her, expecting her to move away from me, as she did before. But she stays put, putting up her hands as a protective wall to suppress any visible reaction to my intrusion of her personal space. I know it gets to her. I can see the nervous flutter of her eyelashes, the fast paced breathing, and the blushing cheeks. Her eyes are still locked on mine, and I admire her for that because I know she'd love nothing more than to evade my gaze. It would make coming up with rational decisions so much easier.

But she's trapped now. She's trying to be brave, and I'm here to make sure she'll lose her battle of conscience.

"Because I invited you for drinks at my place," I say. "And I think it's very impolite of you to decline."

She tenses up and her breathing accelerates, while her lips part as if she's calling out for me. It's so fucking inviting. My cock twitches, eager to be buried inside of her.

I need to taste. I won't let her go anywhere without claiming a taste of those pouty lips that are calling out to me.

She flinches when I move even closer to her, placing the tip of my finger beneath her chin to tilt her face up to mine.

"You don't want to be impolite, do you?" I whisper, my face so close to hers that I can feel her breath on my lips.

She shakes her head.

CHAPTER XI

Elodie

I can't fight it. I can't resist him.

When Kingston Abrams presses his lips on mine it feels as if he takes everything from me. He strips me of my ability to fight, of every ounce of air, to push him away the way I should. He claims me with a passionate kiss, and instead of pressing my lips shut and denying him access, I welcome him in with a soft sigh.

He invades my mouth with a forcefulness that is completely out of line.

So damn alluring.

And so forbidden.

We can't. We shouldn't. This is so wrong.

I tell my brain to shut up for a few moments and close my eyes to indulge in the moment. I have never been kissed like this before. Hungry, sensual, demanding. It's as if he's just slipped me the sweetest drug, fogging my sanity and causing me to cast aside any sort of reason.

I lose hold of the bag with my sheets when he suddenly wraps his arms around my body to pull me closer. The bag falls to the floor and the flutter of paper announces my sheets of music spreading all over the floor beneath our feet.

I don't care.

He pulls me against him and I'm met with a wall of muscle. He's holding me in such a tight clasp, I couldn't leave if I wanted to, while his other hand travels along the side of my body, wandering upward until it finds the side of my breast. I moan in pain when he gropes it through the thin fabric of my blouse.

Shit, shit, shit. What is happening?

My core is clenching, a tingly feeling acting as the harbinger of lust.

What is he doing to me?

While our tongues continue to intertwine, I helplessly lift my arms to touch him, but he won't let me. The moment my hands land on his rock-hard back, he lets go of me and withdraws to grab my wrists and push my hands down.

"No," he says, casting me a warning look.

That's all. For a moment, I fear that this was it, that he tricked me, that I've lost my job and any other opportunity that might have come from this.

But his lips are back on mine within a few seconds, his strong hands still holding on to mine and keeping them pushed down to the side of my body, while he claims me with another kiss.

I'm completely at his mercy, helpless and stunned with desire. Being kissed like this comes close to torture. We're both breathing as if we're racing, our tongues still dancing passionately, while I can feel every part of my body heating up.

I want to feel him, to touch his muscular chest, his face, his everything. But the grip he has on me is unbreakable.

A disappointed sigh escapes my lips when he retreats and ends our kiss.

I open my eyes and am instantly ashamed at my behavior. His grip doesn't loosen one bit and I'm still incapable of moving my arms.

"How about those drinks now?" he asks, a confident smirk on his handsome face.

I'm panting like a bitch in heat, and just now realize that my mouth is still partly opened.

"You're engaged," I breathe, as if that was news to either one of us. "What the hell are you doing?"

He shakes his head.

"I told you, beautiful Elodie, not everything is always as it seems," he says. "You have nothing to worry about."

"Yes, I do!" I insist. "I can't −"

"Hush, hush," he says, placing his index finger on my lips. "Trust me."

Trust him? How can I trust a man like him?

"I don't trust cheaters," I whisper, despite his finger still on my lips.

I want to suck on that finger, and I blush at the thought of it, fueled with a mixture of embarrassment and anger.

He frowns at me and traces along the line of my jaw, traveling down to my neck. His fingertip is barely caressing my skin, but the shivers his touch sends through my body are so intense that it's almost unbearable.

"It's not cheating when there's no love," he says. "Wouldn't you agree?"

Our eyes meet and I hope to God that the sincerity I see in his is not pure imagination.

"No love?" I ask.

His finger trails along my collarbone before he moves back to my neck and places his hand there, holding me in a strong grip at the back of my neck.

"No love," he repeats. "That's not what this is about."

I furl my eyebrows, unsure what he's talking about when he says 'this'. His engagement? About what is happening between us right now?

Probably both.

I long for nothing more than to continue that kiss. I find myself leaning forward, silently begging for him to do what he did before and take the control away from me.

But he doesn't do it this time. Instead, his eyes are locked on mine, searching for approval.

I'm torn between my agonizing desire for him and the rational voice that tells me to get out of this while I still can.

He's so freaking off limits. It could destroy everything. My reputation, my career, his impending marriage. However, I have to admit that the latter is the least of my concerns.

"You don't love Gloria," I say. It was supposed to be a question, but it came out as a statement.

He takes his time to give me a reply. For what feels like an eternity, he just looks at me, his eyes narrow and his gaze intense, while the machinery behind his forehead is working at full speed.

He's either lying or uncomfortable with confirming the truth, if what he's implying is true.

"I don't love Gloria," he validates. "And she doesn't love me."

"That's sad," I say, biting my tongue. I'm usually not this straightforward, let alone judgmental.

"Most of all, it's true," he retorts. "That is all you need to know for now."

He places another kiss on my lips, just an innocent peck before he straightens up.

"Come, have a drink with me," he repeats his offer.

I almost say yes. My core is still trembling, my heart still racing, and my cheeks still flushed. I'm dizzy with lust, and if I'd allow myself to follow the dangerous thoughts and ideas that draw me toward him, I'd agree in an instant.

Luckily, I'm smarter than that.

I clear my throat and distance myself from him.

"No," I say, shaking my head. "I have to go home."

I don't wait for him to reply, but hurry to gather my sheets of music from the floor. After watching me for a few moments, he goes down on his knees next to me and collects a few of my sheets, piling them up in a neat stack before he hands them over to me.

Our eyes meet when I take them, and I almost regret my decision when I see the disappointment reflected in the depth of his dark gray eyes. He's not mad, or at least he doesn't show it. He just looks like someone who had to accept a setback.

However, he doesn't look like someone who's about to give up.

CHAPTER XII

Elodie

"**N**o session at the Abrams' residence today?" my roommate Kim asks when she sees me lounging on my bed as she enters the room.

I lazily turn my head toward her.

"Not today," I say, even though she has good reason to ask. Even though my encounter with Kingston left me unraveled and confused, I continue to practice in the family's music room as often as possible. I've been there three times since that sinful kiss, but Kingston has never shown up again. It was either his mother or Wally who would open the door for me, and both women seem to enjoy my company.

"It's so nice to hear you play while I clean," Wally once told me. "The house is so empty and lonely most of the time."

I feel most comfortable when it's just her and me in the vast and luxurious house. Wally doesn't eye me the way the home-owners do. She doesn't make me feel out of place or under-dressed in any way.

Mrs. Abrams never said anything about my appearance, but the mere contrast between her and me is a painful reminder of how different our lives are. She's very polite, but in a distant way. Yet, she's very insistent on letting me know that I'm welcome to practice as often as I need, and she never lets me leave without telling her when I'll be back next. She appears to be a busy woman, even though it's a mystery to me what could possibly keep her so occupied.

She's so nice to me, which makes what happened between me and Kingston all the worse for me. I feel as if I've betrayed her trust. She may like me for our Juilliard connection and the fact that I remind her of a time in her life that's long gone, but obviously had a significant impact on her. If she knew that I kissed her soon-to-be-married son...

Or that he kissed me. He was the one who started it. I just didn't stop the kiss. At least I managed to avoid things from going any farther than that.

Kim throws her bag in the small corner that's on her side of the room and drops down on her chair, facing me.

"What are they like?" she wants to know.

"Who?" I ask, sitting up on my bunk bed. "The Abrams family?"

"Yeah," Kim says, nodding. "I've heard so much about them and the Waldorf family. I just wonder how much of it is true."

"Heard so much about them?" I wonder. "Like what?"

Kim is just about to answer my question, when she pauses and glances over to our door. She gets up and walks over to close it, before she gets back on her chair and looks at me through wide eyes.

"I mean, it's just gossip, you know. They're big names on the Upper East Side, old money families with strong ties to everyone who's rich and important. A lot of Juilliard teachers and students have performed in those circles."

I shrug. "Yes, I've heard."

"Yeah, but I bet you don't know this..."

She pauses and leans forward, casting me a conspirational look.

"Like, one girl from my orchestra has worked for the Waldorfs recently," she continues, now with a lowered voice, as if she was afraid someone could hear us. "It was ridiculous, she said. One of the Waldorf brats had a birthday party and asked for a private solo violin concert."

"One of the daughters?" I ask. "Was her name Gloria?"

Kim shakes her head.

"No, someone younger," she says. "Isn't Gloria Waldorf the girl you're playing for? The bride-to-be?"

I nod. "Yes, that's why I was wondering."

"Well, it wasn't her. Maybe her younger sister? Or a cousin? In any case, she was at the party," Kim recounts. "I know she was there, because so was her fiancé, what's his face Abrams —"

"Kingston," I interject. "His name is Kingston."

Kim nods enthusiastically and points her finger up in the air. "Yes, exactly! Kingston! I heard he's quite the looker? Super handsome and fit and stuff?"

I blush and hope to God that Kim doesn't notice it. If she does, she doesn't say anything about it.

"Yeah, he's good looking," I say, making the understatement of the year. "But she's very pretty, too."

Kim huffs.

"Aren't they all?" she says. "Those rich kids... Well, anyway. My friend, you know, the violinist, she said that at that birthday party, she heard Gloria talking to one of her friends and... oh my God, swear to me you won't tell anyone?"

I furl my eyebrows. "Don't tell anyone what?"

"She's sleeping with other guys!" Kim exclaims. "Like, at the time of the birthday party, Gloria and Kingston were already an item, it was shortly before they announced their engagement, so not too long ago. But my friend said that after her performance she was invited to stick around and have a drink or something, and that's when she heard Gloria bragging to her friends about all the different guys she was sleeping with."

Not everything is as it seems.

His words are ringing in my ears. Kingston has told me that there was no love between them, and he might have suggested that there was no commitment either. I just didn't want to hear it.

I arch my eyebrows, trying to act more shocked at the revelation than I actually am.

"Are you sure?" I ask. "She's cheating on him?"

Kim nods. "Big time! And her friends didn't even seem to be appalled or anything. It's so weird! They all acted as if it was the most normal thing in the world."

I lower my eyes. "Well, I guess to some people it is."

"To those people, maybe," Kim says. "It's so disgusting. Like in the old times, when people just got married to unite two different kingdoms."

"That could be it," I presume.

"Ugh," Kim makes, shaking her head with disgust. "How sick. My friend said that while Gloria was very open about it among her friends, she made them swear not to talk about it with anyone else, especially their parents. So it's kind of an open secret and everybody just acts as if this was a normal wedding, a real wedding, you know, between two people who love each other, when it's really just some kind of deal."

She pauses and contemplates for a few moments, before she giggles. "Oh man, they have to produce heirs, too. I wonder how they get that done?"

"Do you think he sleeps around, too?" I ask, surprised at myself. "Kingston, I mean. Her fiancé."

Kim regards me with a look of surprise.

"Obviously," she says. "He's known to be one of the worst players ever. My friend said that she actually felt sorry for Gloria, before she heard her talk like that on the party, because the rumors about him are so bad."

"What rumors?" I want to know.

Kim looks at me as if that was dumbest question she's ever heard.

"Have you been living under a rock?" she asks.

I frown at her. "No? Maybe I just don't have as much time as other people to engage in gossip."

"Yeah, yeah," Kim says, waving me off. "But everybody has heard about the Abrams sons, both of them. I have no idea why that guy, Kingston, would even agree to marry. Maybe he's being forced somehow? He has a terrible reputation as an asshole heart breaker, dropping girls left and right after lying his head off."

Kim pauses and looks at me through narrow eyes.

"You've met him, right?" she wants to know.

I try acting as unfazed as possible. "Yes, once. The first time I introduced myself to the family."

"Oh," she says. "Well, watch out. Apparently he doesn't even shy away from people who work for him or his family. I heard that one of his father's interns had to quit because of him."

I prick up my ears. "She had to quit? Why?"

Kim shrugs. "Because they hooked up, it became public information, no one batted an eye about him, but she was suddenly considered a slut and people started talking behind her back, suggesting that she only hooked up with him to have an advantage or something."

"Oh," I say, trying to hide the cold shower of fright traveling down my spine.

"It's so unfair!" Kim exclaims. "Boys like him get to do whatever they want and they're celebrated as heroes, the cool players. And girls? We get slut-shamed if we're just looking for a little fling."

Our eyes meet and she gasps as she suddenly remembers.

"Well, you know what I'm talking about," she says, lowering her voice. "After what happened with Benjamin."

I furl my eyebrows.

"Do I?" I ask. "Are people talking about that?"

Kim clears her throat and slowly shakes her head. "Not really. Not people..."

I sit up on my bed and lean down to her.

"Did you hear anything?" I want to know. "Why would anyone talk about me that way? Who would even care?"

"Benjamin," she says, looking at me like a kid who got caught in the act because she just spilled the beans on something she was supposed to keep to herself.

"Benjamin?" I repeat. "What would *he* say? We just hooked up a few times. It was nothing. That would barely qualify me as a slut!"

Kim shakes her head.

"No, of course not!" she agrees. "And I don't agree with him at all! But, he's just... hurt, you know? I mean, you do know."

I nod. "Yeah, he didn't take it that well."

"Oh, I shall say," Kim says. "I didn't want to tell you because I don't think anyone is listening to him anyway, but he... well, he's been spreading some stuff about you. I don't think it's true! And like I said, I don't even think anyone even listens to him and –"

"What has he been saying?" I ask, jumping from my bed. My heart is racing with fury.

Kim sighs. "Oh, boy, I shouldn't have mentioned it..."

"Kim," I urge. "What has he been saying about me?"

"Ugh, nothing really, it's nonsense –"

"Kim, please!" I screech.

"Well, he kinda' said that you lied to him," she finally says. "He said that you lead him on to believe that you were in love with him, so that he'd commit to you."

I shrug.

"So?" I ask. "That's a lie, a very bad one at that. Doesn't sound too bad."

"And he also said that you cheated on him," Kim continues. "And that you were sleeping around with several guys, and even... took money from some of them."

"What?!" I yell. "He said *what*?!"

Kim flinches and tries to hush me.

"Really, Elodie, I wouldn't worry about it, no one believes him anyway," she says, raising her hand in a defensive gesture, trying to calm me down.

"Kim, this is *not* funny," I say with a quavering voice. "He's telling people that I prostitute myself!"

"He's a loser, Elodie," Kim says. "It's an obvious lie, everyone knows that."

"But you of all people know how gossip works," I say. "However ridiculous and unbelievable it may be, rumors like that spread like wildfire, and eventually there are going to be enough people who actually believe that stuff and then –"

"No, no," Kim interrupts me. "That's impossible, Elodie. I'm positive that won't happen."

I'm so furious that I could cry. But I realize that Kim is not the person who deserves my anger right now. After all, she's just the messenger.

"When did you first hear about it?" I ask her.

She looks at me through wide eyes.

"I don't know," she says. "A few days ago?"

And here I was thinking that the only person who could endanger my reputation would be Kingston Abrams and his seductive ways.

How could Benjamin do this to me? I don't deserve this.

"I've got to talk to him," I whisper, more to myself than to Kim.

"He's gone for the week," Kim reminds me. "Some kind of workshop upstate."

"Of course, he is," I sigh. I reach up to my bed and grab my phone from the little shelf next to my cushion. While I may not be able to confront the asshole upfront, I need to let him know that I'm aware of his pathetic display.

CHAPTER XIII

Kingston

I know her schedule. Elodie shows up at my parents' home three times a week now, every Monday, Tuesday and Friday. Those are the afternoons and evenings when she doesn't have classes and doesn't have to work at her part time job.

I don't have a habit of dropping by my childhood home all that often, so it's not hard to stay out of her way. I haven't given up on her, though. That's not what I do. I'm not a quitter.

However, I'm not getting anywhere with her. That kiss. Those lips. She tasted fantastic, and she welcomed my invasion like a good girl. I could feel her slim and innocent body under my hands, shivering and burning for me.

That sigh when I confined her hands to the side of her body...

And then it stopped.

She put an end to it and was out of my sight within seconds. She fled out the door, and I didn't follow her or even ask to drive her home.

I just let her go.

And I've been avoiding her ever since.

My gaze darkens as I fixate on the drink in my hands. I'm sitting at my parents' dinner table with Gloria at my side. We're alone because neither my father nor my mother has blessed us with their presence yet.

"It's unusual for them to make us wait," Gloria says, casting a glance at her wristwatch.

"Not really," I say, remembering a thousand instances when my parents would play the diva card and show up whenever it fit their schedule.

Gloria sighs. "Well, they've never left *me* waiting."

I ignore her and take another sip from my drink. Whisky, from an aged triple cask. Only the best stuff is served at my parents' house and Wally knows exactly what I like. She's rummaging in the kitchen, adding the final touches to our dinner. Our weekly dinner is one of the many obligations that force Gloria and me to act like a real couple, even if it's only in front of our parents, two people who should understand how fake our relationship really is.

In a way, they probably see it as practice for us. If we learn to behave like a normal couple, like two people who are in love, it would help us maintain our ruse. I'm fairly certain that a part of them hopes we might actually fall in love if we're forced to spend this much time together. As far as I'm concerned, the fact that my parents keep us waiting right now is nothing but another attempt at creating a situation that forces Gloria and me to interact with each other.

"Heard you were seen at the club last weekend," Gloria says, looking at me through her thickly painted lashes.

"Heard?" I ask. "From whom?"

She huffs. "My guys. You know I have friends everywhere. Listen Kingston, I'm not stupid. But you should really be more careful."

She looks at me with a snarky face. "What kind of image does that convey? You, out and about on the weekend, picking up some dumb bimbos while your poor fiancée is waiting for you at home?"

Now I'm the one huffing. The thought of Gloria sitting home alone, waiting for me to come to her to snuggle up under the covers, it's just too ridiculous.

"I highly doubt that's what you were doing," I say taking another sip from my drink.

She chuckles.

"Of course not," she pipes. "But unlike you, I'm smart enough to play out my little adventures in private, behind closed doors. Not in plain sight for everybody to see."

I don't even want to know. I don't care about her exploits, and I don't even know if she has many interchangeable lovers at the moment or just one steady guy. It doesn't concern me at all and I don't care.

"For everybody to see," I repeat, shaking my head. "Sorry, Gloria, I think you overestimate our celebrity status. No one cares about our private lives that much."

"That's not true," she says, shaking her head like a teacher responding to a student who just gave the wrong answer to one of her questions. "There are a lot of people who care, and it would hurt our reputation if —"

"Whatever," I interrupt her. "None of them are hanging out at the same places where I like to spend my nights. And who the fuck cares about rumors?"

"You should care!" she hisses. "Your reputation is bad enough already. No one wants to do business with an idiotic whippersnapper who can't control his dick and fucks around like a horny teenager. You're about to take over your father's position for God's sake, and I'm helping you do so. You better help us by making this work."

"You're not doing this to help me," I snap at her. "You're doing this because you want your parents to get off your back and to be left alone and free to continue carrying on with your parties and lovers."

We glare at each other, disgusted by one another just as much as by ourselves.

Luckily, my parents choose this moment to finally make an appearance in the dining room.

"Oh, we're sorry to make you wait," my mother coos, completely oblivious to the infuriated tension between us.

"Don't worry about it," Gloria says, beaming at my mother. "We were just talking about the engagement party."

She smiles at me, and I really have to keep it together not to let anyone see how much her fake attitude disgusts me.

"It's getting closer," my father says, as he pulls out the chair for my mother to sit.

"Are you getting excited?" my mother asks, smiling at Gloria and then at me. It's obvious that there's only one answer she'll accept.

"Yes, very," Gloria says, her voice so high-pitched that it hurts my ears.

While they engage in their girlish small talk, my mind wanders back to the only feature of our engagement party that excites me: the pianist.

Sweet, innocent Elodie and her erotic expressions while she plays. She is driving me nuts and I don't see how I'm supposed to get through that ludicrous event if I haven't had her yet. I might attack and ravage her that night, during her performance, while everyone watches.

Fuck, how I'd love that. Her horrified eyes, her cheeks blushed while I force her to ride my cock.

This has to happen. And it *will* happen.

I just don't know how yet.

Our dinner is served, and halfway through the entree, my attention returns to the conversation at the table, as I hear Elodie's name mentioned.

"She's a talented artist, that girl," my mother praises her. "And so diligent. She works very hard on cultivating that talent of hers; it's quite admirable."

"Absolutely," my father agrees, even though I'm sure he barely listened to my mother's exact words. He doesn't care about Elodie one bit, but he's all about diligence and hard work. My entire upbringing is proof of that.

"And to come from such dire circumstances," my mother continues. "She certainly wasn't born with a silver spoon in her mouth."

Gloria huffs. "Yeah, one could tell, with her clothes basically falling apart when she first showed up here."

My mother doesn't say anything, but regards her with a warning look.

"Dire circumstances?" I ask.

My mother turns to me, arching her eyebrows in a gesture of empathy.

"Oh, yes, I talked to her teacher for a bit when I first inquired about a student to hire," she says. "She has no mother, and the father... well, let's just say he doesn't exactly rely on liquid poison in moderation. I don't think she can expect anything from him when it comes to supporting her education. She has a scholarship."

"And a part-time job," I add.

All eyes turn to me.

"Yes," my mother says, her eyes wide in surprise. "How did you know?"

I shrug. "Just an assumption."

Gloria's eyes stay on me a little longer than I feel comfortable with. She may be hateful, but she's not stupid. If anyone ever finds out about my interest in Elodie, I'm sure she'd be the first one. If I have a choice, I'd like to prevent that from happening.

"In any case, we shouldn't mock her for her poverty," my mother adds. "Especially when she's working so hard on getting somewhere with her talent."

My father nods quietly.

I don't let it show, but my mother's words sparked an idea inside my head that could endear myself to Elodie – or end in an absolute catastrophe. It's perfect. No risk, no fun.

"We should really consider taking her on for the wedding reception, as well," my mother continues singing her praise of Elodie. "And the rehearsal dinner, if that requires music."

"I don't mind," Gloria says. "It would be easier than having to look for someone else. Right, Kingston?"

The way she looks at me suggests nothing good. I reciprocate her look without showing any sign of emotion.

"Right," I agree.

CHAPTER XIV

Elodie

"There's a package for you," Kim announces when I bump into her in our apartment. She's on her way out, while I just came back from class to change before I get on my way over to the Abrams' residence to practice.

"I put it on your table," Kim adds, as she rushes past me.

"A package for me?" I ask, bewildered.

She stops with her hand on the doorknob and turns back to me.

"Yeah," she says. "You weren't expecting anything?"

I shake my head. "I never get mail."

"I know!" she says. "I was surprised, too! Sorry, really gotta' go!"

She waves goodbye and is out the door a moment later.

I hurry to our room and find a big box on my table.

"What the...?" I whisper, leaving my door open as I approach my desk next to the window.

This must be a mistake. I don't have anyone who'd send me mail, let alone a huge box such as this one. No one in my family has the money for gifts, and I don't have any friends outside school. It's not my birthday either, and I'm pretty sure that I didn't do any online shopping lately. I have no extra money for that.

The box takes up pretty much the entire surface of my desk, but it's not as heavy as I expected it to be. I lift it up and turn it around, searching for the name of the sender, but there's none. How is that even possible? Isn't that obligatory? However, it is indeed addressed to me.

I fetch a knife from our kitchen and return to the room to open the box. The first thing inside that catches my attention is a beautiful envelope, decorated with golden lines at the edges. There's just one word written on the front of it: my name, Elodie.

My hands are shaking when I open the envelope. For some reason, I can only imagine bad things to happen next. Benjamin is still gone, but maybe he's sent me something mean to give voice to his rotten feelings toward me? I don't recognize his handwriting on the envelope, but he's the only person I can think of right now.

Until I read the note inside the envelope. It doesn't say much, only a few, sweet words.

"You deserve better, beautiful."

That's it. No name, no identification of the sender.

I blush and frown simultaneously. Who is this from? Who'd think that I deserve better? Better than what?

I put the note aside and rummage through the box. There are a bunch of smaller packages wrapped in white and golden wrapping paper, and at the very bottom I find two shoe boxes.

Clothes. These must be clothes.

I rip the first package open and find the most beautiful merino cardigan I've ever touched, and judging from the Gucci tag inside the neck, it's probably the most expensive piece of clothing I've ever held in my hands, too. The entire box is filled with high-end brand name clothing, including three silk blouses that are somehow similar to the one I was wearing the other day while playing piano at the Abrams' home, except the fabric feels a lot thicker and softer. There's one pair of black pants and a pencil skirt, and both would go well with the blouses and the merino cardigan.

Then, there's the dress. My heart almost stops beating when I unpack the light beige Valentino dress. It has a similar cut to the one I wore when I introduced myself to the Abrams and Waldorf families, but that's where the similarities end. Its dignified appearance, finished with eyelash edges and the beautiful lace around the décolleté, stands in no comparison to the dress I own. This must have cost a fortune!

One of the shoe boxes contains Louboutin heels in a light beige that matches the dress, while the other box holds black ballerina slippers that are more suitable for everyday life and could be worn with everything else that I found in the box.

Did they send me this stuff? Is this the family's way of telling me that I should dress for the occasion when I show up at their house? Did I embarrass them, even though no one ever sees me there except for Wally and Mrs. Abrams?

Well, and *him*.

Did Kingston send me all this stuff? Why? What the hell is he thinking? I can't be bought, and if I start running around in these clothes, the ugly rumors that Benjamin has been trying to spread around about me would only gain credibility.

I can't accept this.

But I kind of want to.

I longingly hold up one of the blouses in front of me. It's so exquisite! The texture, the cut, the color. Everything about it is perfect. I've never had pretty things like this.

I reckon that it can't hurt to try it on, just to see what it looks like. I lock myself in my room and go through the box item by item, starting with one of the blouses and the pants. Luckily, Kim and I have a full-size mirror in our room, so that I can get a pretty good look at every outfit. Every single piece fits perfectly, even the most valuable thing, the dress, which I try on last.

The dress is perfect for performance, but I'm not sure about the matching heels. I've never played the piano wearing heels like that, and I imagine it could be challenging to control the pedal with them.

In any case, I'm not going to try this out tonight. It's getting late and I really need to get going, so I can make good use of my practicing hours on the grand piano. Today is one of the days when no one but Wally will be around, and she must already be expecting me.

There's only one question left to answer before I can leave. Do I choose an outfit out of this box or opt for the dark jeans and crimson top I was going to wear?

My eyes rest on the pretty clothes lying spread out on my bed. If no one but Wally sees me tonight, it doesn't really matter what I wear. I could show up in ripped jeans and I doubt she would bat an eye. Unless she's instructed to report back to Mrs. Abrams, if she was the one to send this box to me. But something tells me that she's not the sender. Why would she make a secret about being the one who gave these incredible gifts to me? No, it must be Kingston, and I'm deadset on returning everything to him.

But until then, I might as well take them out once. Just for fun, just for myself.

CHAPTER XV

Kingston

She's wearing the cream-colored bow tie blouse and the skirt, paired up with the black ballerina shoes and the merino cardigan to protect herself from the cold. Everything looks just as delicious and perfect on her as I imagined, and it is only topped by her beautifully surprised face.

She stares up at me through wide eyes, her lips forming a small O as she inhales audibly upon seeing me opening the door for her.

"Hello, Elodie," I say. "Here to play, are you?"

She blushes and absentmindedly reaches up to her throat to tug at the collar of her blouse.

"What are you doing here?" she asks. "Where's Wally?"

"Wally is already done for the day," I say, causing Elodie to erupt in insecurity.

"Am I that late?" she asks. "I'm so sorry, I didn't –"

"No, you're not late," I say, beckoning for her to come inside. "You look lovely."

She hesitates and remains standing outside, holding on to her shoulder bag, the only accessory that doesn't go with the rest of her outfit.

"Did you send me this?" she asks shyly.

I smile at her. "You look even better than I imagined."

Elodie evades my eyes, but finally decides to come inside. I close the door behind her and am met with her questioning eyes when I turn around.

"Why?" she asks.

"You're welcome," I say, raising my eyebrow at her.

She clears her throat.

"Yes, thank you," she says. "But I want to know why? And I will also let you know that I don't intend to keep any of it."

"Why are you wearing it then?" I ask.

She sighs. "I didn't think anyone would see. I thought Wally would –"

"So?" I interrupt her. "You're just having trouble admitting that you like it?"

"I..." she gasps as I take a step closer to her and lift my hand up to her face. Elodie's green eyes widen, but she doesn't shy away when I gently caress along her cheek and tug a strand of hair behind her naked ears. Almost perfect, but she needs jewelry. Small pearl earrings would go nicely with this. I make a mental note to take care of it.

I lean forward to steal another kiss from her. It's a bold move, but not too bold for naughty little Elodie. She closes her eyes, as if she wants to submit all the responsibility to me. Very promising. I let her know how hungry I am for her, not wasting a second on reluctance and caution. She needs to know how much I need to taste her. I invade her mouth with voracious need, placing my hand at the back of her neck to keep her in place.

She welcomes me just as she did last time, but eventually starts gasping for air, lifting her hands up as if to declare defeat. I notice that she wants to touch me, but she doesn't do it.

What a good girl.

I end our kiss, leaving her panting and staring at me with wanting eyes.

"Why?" she repeats her question, but this time it seems to be directed at more than just my generous present.

"I told you why," I say. "Because you deserve better."

Tears start to pool in the corners of her eyes. "What makes you say that? You hardly know me."

"Just a feeling," I say, smirking at her. "And my feelings are usually right."

She shakes her head and reaches up to my hand at her back, about to move it away.

"You don't know me," she repeats.

"Then let me get to know you," I reply.

Now she openly frowns at me.

"You don't want to get to know me," she says. "I know what you want. I'm not stupid."

I'm sure she's not, but she's wrong about one thing. I do want to get to know her. Her innocent beauty was what drew me toward her in the beginning, but it has become so much more to me now. There is something about her that I can't ignore. Something new, something mysterious and foreign to me. I need to find out what it is, I need to be able to touch it.

And I fucking need to see her bend over for me.

"You don't know me either," I interject.

She rolls her eyes – something I will not forget – and arches her left eyebrow.

"I've heard enough about you to know what this is," she says.

"Oh, you've heard about me?" I inquire. "So, this judgment is based on gossip and people talking behind my back?"

I shake my head, acting as if I was disappointed. "I never thought you'd be so shallow, Elodie."

She inhales with indignation.

"I'm not shallow!" she insists. "But I'm also not stupid enough to get involved in your sick little world."

"My sick little world?"

"Yes," she says. "Your sick little world of fake marriages, adultery, cheating and lies. I have enough drama going on in my life as is, I don't need to add this kind of –"

"Hold on, hold on!" I interrupt her, squeezing her dainty little neck. "What are you talking about?"

She bites her lower lip and hisses, "Never mind."

"Oh, but I do mind," I say. "I don't know what you've heard, Elodie, and quite frankly, I don't care. All you need to focus on is this."

I point back and forth between me and her.

"You feel it, I know you do. There's heat, there's tension, there's something drawing us to each other," I continue, now caressing her cheek with the other hand while still holding her at the neck. She shivers under my touch.

"You feel it," I whisper. "And you want to explore this, don't you?"

She looks up at through teary eyes.

"This is not about what I want," she breathes.

"Yes, it is," I object.

She tries to shake her head, but I don't let her.

"Please," she whispers, closing her eyes. "Please, don't get me in trouble."

My chest tenses up at her words. There it is. Her fright, her distrust. She thinks I'm going to use her and rat her out.

"Elodie," I say. "I don't want to hurt you."

This much is true. There's no way for me to prove it, but the thought of hurting her, of putting her name and reputation in danger, that just makes me sick. I want to fuck her, explore that delicious body of hers, use her in my own way, see that beautiful face erupt with emotion because of me and not because of a song she's playing.

That's what I want.

I lean closer to her.

"I want to taste you," I whisper. "All of you. I want to fuck you the way you need it. I want to fuck you in a way you've never been fucked before, I want to see you explode with lust under my touch, and I want to be responsible for you to lose control. I want to see you the way I saw you playing your music, but I want to be better for you than any song could ever be."

Her lips are quivering, and I can feel the heat on her rosy cheeks. She's mine. I've got her right where I want her.

She just needs to realize it.

Elodie clears her throat.

"But Gloria and —"

"You know very damn well what Gloria means to me, what this engagement means to me," I say. "And what it means to her. We have our reasons for doing this, but love isn't one of them."

"What then?" she wants to know.

I shake my head.

"You don't need to know that now," I say. "All you need to know is that you can trust me. Whatever happens between us will remain our dirty little secret. I have as little interest in any of this getting out to the world as you do."

Our eyes are locked onto each other while she tries to gather her thoughts. I can see clarity in hers for one second, and confusion and panic the next. Just as I fear that I might be losing her again, she opens her pretty little mouth.

"Okay," she whispers. "I trust you."

I smile at her, knowing that I've won.

"So, do you think you could skip today's piano practice?" I ask her.

She smiles. "I've never skipped a practice before, unless I've had to work."

"Well, you could consider this part of your job," I say, planting a kiss on her lips.

"You're just getting to know your client a little better."

CHAPTER XVI

Elodie

O h my God, what am I doing?

I could lose my job over this, but yet I can't stop my heart from doing somersaults as Kingston drives me to his place. I don't even know where he lives, just that it's somewhere close to the river and not too far from his parents' place.

"I can't be home too late," I say, sounding like a teenager. Neither of us has spoken since we got inside the car and I can no longer bear the awkward silence because it leaves too much room for me to think.

He chuckles. "Why? Will you get in trouble with the warden?"

I cast him an annoyed look from the side.

"I have a long day tomorrow, starting with an early class, practice, my part-time job and —"

"Alright, alright," he says, raising his hand to stop my worrisome lamenting. "I told you, you can trust me. Let's put those worries aside for tonight, okay?"

He looks at me then, winking and looking way too handsome for me to object. Benjamin always blamed me for being too cold, too distant and emotionally unavailable, even before I ended things between us. Sometimes I wish these things were true because it would mean that I have a lot more experience with things like this than what I actually do. Maybe then I could be cooler and more nonchalant about this whole situation.

I'm about to do something bad, something wrong and dangerous, that could blew up in my face big time.

The ride to Kingston's place seems painfully long, and I feel like I'm watching a movie where the protagonist is about to make a huge mistake. I'm sitting in the audience, yelling and protesting, telling the girl not to be so stupid.

Yet, here I am. I am that girl, and I am about to make this mistake because I feel I deserve it. My life has been nothing but work and piano practice for years, only spiced with the occasional hookup with random fellow students, and none of those hookups ever left me with a good feeling. On the contrary.

This could be different. Kingston is different from the boys I've fooled around with before. He's not that much older, but he radiates a maturity that attracts me to no end.

Also, he's rich, he wants to treat me to indulgences that are reserved for the kinds of people I work typically for. And damn it, I deserve a treat! At least with him, I won't have to worry about hurt feelings on his part.

"Are you okay?" he asks, pulling me out of my stream of thoughts. I didn't realize that I was staring at him the whole time, my fingers clenching around the bag on my lap. I must have looked like a witch who was concocting an evil spell of some sort.

"Yes, sorry," I say, turning my eyes back to focus on the street ahead of us.

"Don't excuse yourself for looking at me," he tells me. "But I'd love to know what you were thinking."

"Nothing," I hurry to reply.

"That's a lie," he insists. "Don't lie to me, Elodie. I have enough of that going on in my life."

I can't tell if he's mocking me because of what I said earlier, or if he's actually trying to give me an insight into his own weird life.

"You don't like to be lied to?" I ask.

He shakes his head. "No one does."

"But... aren't you doing it all the time?" I quickly follow up. "To Gloria, your family, everyone."

He regards me with a quick glance from the side. "Only when it's necessary."

"Why do you live a life where it is necessary to lie?" I ask him.

My eyes are fixated on him, but he doesn't reciprocate the look, instead keeping his eyes trained straight ahead on the street in front of us.

"You don't know me and my life, Elodie. Stop the judging," he says.

I've never been accused of being judgmental. If anything, I was the one who'd accuse other people of doing it. I inhale audibly, trying to find the right words to defend myself, but I fail miserably. How do you defend yourself against an accusation you've bestowed upon others numerous times before?

"Sorry," I say instead, surprised at myself. "I didn't mean to judge."

"People usually don't mean to," he says. "I never understood why that's an acceptable excuse. 'I didn't mean to'. If you don't mean to do it, just don't do it in the first place."

Jeez, he can be sensitive. However, he does have a point.

"I just said it for lack of words," I try to explain myself. "I couldn't think of anything else to say."

"I know," he says, and stops the car.

Up until now, I hadn't even noticed that he had entered a driveway in front of a modern high-rise building with a glass facade.

He keeps the motor running and jumps out of the car so quickly that I can barely react before the door on my side opens. A middle-aged man in a uniform who looks like a doorman at one of those expensive five star hotels beckons me to get out of the car, and I follow his gesture, only to be greeted by Kingston who just made his way over to my side. He takes my hand, which is unnecessary because I'm already out of the car, but I don't fight it. His touch is weirdly familiar and gentle, and he shows no intention of wanting to let go of my hand any time soon.

"Thanks, Glen," Kingston says, his statement directed at the guy who opened the door for me, before he leads me toward the entrance, still holding my hand.

"Does he work for you?" I ask another dumb question.

"Not only for me," Kingston says. "Everybody in this building. I'm no prince, Elodie."

I cast a look around the entrance lobby of the high-rise building. White marble decor, floor-to-ceiling windows, and light gray floor tiles that I assume are made of expensive marble, as well. There's a reception area with another man sitting behind the counter. He's dressed in the same uniform as the guy who opened my car door, but he's a few years younger and more sturdily built. He looks more like a fancy bouncer than a doorman. When we walk by, he greets us with a quick nod, casting a look at Kingston first before he regards me with a polite smile.

"You're certainly as rich as a prince," I whisper in passing, trying to push aside the awkward thoughts that arose when the reception guy smiled at me. I can't help but wonder how many girls Kingston has dragged through this entrance. How many girls this month? This week? If what I've heard about him is true, I should have no illusions about not being the first girl that man has smiled at this week.

I wonder if he feels sorry for me. If he thinks that I'm here under false pretenses? A part of me wants to run back to him to tell him that I'm not stupid enough to believe in fairytales, and that I have no illusions, or even the desire, to win over Kingston's heart.

Also, do these men know about Kingston's engagement? They must. Everybody does.

"And this is not a problem?" I mumble, more to myself than to him.

We're standing in front of the elevators and Kingston casts me a confused look.

"What isn't a problem?" he asks.

I look back over my shoulder to see if the man at the reception desk is still looking at us, but he isn't. He has lowered his eyes and appears to be deeply absorbed with something on the desk in front of him.

"To be seen like this, with me," I say, turning back to Kingston. "Do you always bring your girls here?"

He looks at me, his eyes narrowing.

"We need to establish some ground rules," he says, instead of answering my question. "One: no talk of other girls. You are the one I'm with tonight, just you. Stop talking about that silly gossip –"

"It's not just gossip," I hiss, interrupting him. "I don't like lying either, Kingston."

He raises his eyebrows.

"Feisty, I like that," he comments. "Rule number two: no interrupting. Three: no pondering to yourself, speak to me clearly, honestly."

The elevator door opens then and he pulls me inside as quickly as possible. I stand next to him, ready to protest but baffled at the same time, while he enters a code into a panel next to the door before it closes.

"Four," he says as soon as we're shielded from everyone's view. "I'm in command from now on. And if you don't obey, there'll be punishment."

CHAPTER XVII

Kingston

I don't give her any time to respond, but instead silence her with a kiss that leaves no room for questions. She's here, finally. She agreed to enter my refuge, and it's time for her to understand what it means to be mine. I kiss her hungrily, claiming her not only with my tongue, but with both of my hands, greedily pressing her dainty little body against mine, while her arms are trapped between us, holding that damn bag with her beloved music sheets.

She moans desperately and I know only part of it is to complain about my intrusion and the rules I just laid upon her. When I break our kiss to look at her, she gazes up at me with the look of dazed confusion filling her eyes, as if she was high. I bet this girl has never been high on drugs, and I have no interest in sharing that part of my lifestyle with her, but I'll make her high on bliss. This is just the beginning.

She sighs, trying to regain clarity, but I won't let her.

"Listen, Elodie," I whisper. "You're mine now. We've left everything outside, every doubt, every worry. You'll be a good girl from now on, and I promise you, you won't regret it."

She nods. "I'll try."

I want to tell her that trying will hardly be enough, but the doors open just at that moment, announcing our arrival on the uppermost floor. My floor.

Another door shields us from entering my living area, and I type in another code to make it accessible.

"No way!" she gasps behind me as the door opens, revealing the grand area that serves as my living room. "This is where you live? Oh, my God!"

I know it's a sight to behold, and I've always preferred this to the non-existent views from my family's townhouse, but I grew accustomed to it a long time ago. The panoramic windows on the walls opposite the entrance cover the entire length of the living area, and I just now realize that there's an empty spot in which a grand piano would fit perfectly.

I can't help it. Images like this pop into my head without warning whether I want them to or not. Now, as we step inside and I watch Elodie taking in the view of my home for the first time, I can't help but picture her playing here, sitting at a grand piano by the window, immersed in her music with her eyes closed and her naked body swaying to the melody.

I need to make this happen.

"This is like a movie," she breathes, carefully entering my living room and staring out the window. "Wow!"

She walks over to the window, while I take in the sight of her slim silhouette from behind, pondering what to do with her first. My cock is twitching, begging to be buried deep inside of her, but I don't want to rush this. Restraining my hunger for her is part of the fun, she's not the only one in this I like to keep under control.

"Can I offer you a drink?" I ask, and she swirls around, looking at me as if she just remembered that I was here, too.

"Um," she utters, nodding, but unsure what to request.

"Wine? Champagne? Water?" I list. "Tea?"

She smiles. "Champagne sounds nice."

"I agree," I say, my eyes catching the seating area on the other side of the living room. There's a love seat in front of the window with its back facing the city skyline below, providing the perfect place for a sexy scene.

"Sit," I tell her, nodding toward the love seat.

She turns around to look at it, her eyes casting back and forth between me and the small sofa.

"Could I...," she mumbles. "Freshen up a little first?"

She casts me another one of those endearingly coy smiles, and I point toward the hallway that leads away to the bedrooms.

"First door on the left."

"Thanks," she whispers, before disappearing out of my sight.

I grab us two champagne flutes and a bottle of Salon Blanc de Blancs. Based on what little I know about Elodie Hill, I reckon that she's never tasted a Champagne Salon, one of the finest on the market, and I enjoy the thought of being the first one to introduce her to it.

She returns just as I'm filling the second flute, already sitting on the love seat where I intend to have my first real taste of her.

"Sit," I repeat, patting the cushion next to me.

She obeys, fixing her blouse as she sits down next to me and eyeing the bottle in my hand.

"Oh, Champagne Salon?" she remarks, and a hint of anger knocks inside my chest.

"You've had it before?" I want to know.

Her eyes widen and she shakes her head.

"God no," she says. "I've seen people drink it, but I've never had it myself. It's so expensive!"

I smile and hand her the glass. "It's about time then."

She takes the flute in her hand, looking at it as if I just handed her the key to the world.

"Wow," she gasps, examining the luxurious drink in her hand. "This is way too much."

I chuckle and raise my eyebrows at her.

"You're cute," I tell her, raising my glass to clink. "Nothing is too good for a sweet girl like you."

She furls her eyebrows as we touch glasses. "Charmer."

A cheeky remark that she's going to regret later.

I watch her as she brings the flute to her lips, closing her eyes before she tastes the most exquisite champagne in her life. Watching her reaction is a joy in itself. She's so much classier and naturally elegant in a way that I haven't seen on a girl before. There's nothing fake about her, no rehearsed movements, just a girl savoring a delicacy she's never had before. She takes a tiny sip at first, truly tasting the liquid before she swallows, and then she takes another sip.

Champagne Salon is no novelty for me, so I take a big sip, emptying half of my glass before I put it back on the table. I don't plan on drinking a lot tonight, and especially not now. There are other things on my mind.

"Do you like it?" I ask her.

She nods and takes another sip as if she wants to show me just how much she enjoys it. I can tell by the way she sits and carries herself that she's nervous and tense. She holds on to the champagne flute for dear life, while her other hand rests in her lap, seemingly relaxed but her fingers are nervously tugging on the seam of the blouse I bought her. She smiles at me shyly.

"I'm sorry," she says. "I don't know much about champagne and couldn't elaborate. All I can say is that it tastes delicious."

"That's all that matters anyway," I say. "Take another sip and then put the glass down."

I'm speaking these commands to test her, to see how she reacts to being ordered around. So far, it's still hard to know whether it's mere insecurity or a desire to please that causes her to follow my orders without questioning.

It's her face that tells me there might be more behind her compliance. She winks at me, before she takes another sip, a bigger one this time, and then puts the glass down on the coffee table next to mine. She looks at me with expectation, her green eyes posing a question that cannot pass her lips. "Did I do good?"

I nod. "Good girl."

It's that little flicker in her eyes that tells me she's into this, and a lot more. The power is all mine now, she's willingly handed it over to me, and the rush I feel makes it hard not to execute it to the limit.

I need her closer to me. I need to touch her and control her, not only with my words. When I place my hand on her thigh, she flinches ever so slightly, but doesn't shy away. Her breast heaves when I move my hand toward her center, slowly traveling across her thigh, surpassing the seams of her blouse until I reach her lap. I'm barely touching her, but her breathing accelerated as if we were already far beyond this point of first convergence.

"You like being a good girl for me, don't you?" I ask her, trying to catch her eyes with mine, but she's evading me.

"Look at me," I command.

She sighs, but obeys immediately. There's one thing I've learned about her already. Eye contact is not her thing. It's tough for her, and knowing this about Elodie gives me something to work with.

"Sit on my lap," I tell her, and her eyelashes flutter like excited butterflies.

She gets up from her seat, just about to follow my command and straddle me, when I have another idea.

"Actually," I say, stopping her by raising my hand. "Let me take those pants off of you first."

CHAPTER XVIII

Elodie

He sits back on the sofa, placing his arms on the backrest and looking up at me with confident anticipation. He has no doubt that I will do what he just told me to do, that I will take my pants off in front of him just like that.

Turns out, he's right.

I hesitate only for a moment before my hands start unbuttoning my pants as if they were acting on their own, while I kick off my shoes at the same time. My eyes follow their movement, but as soon as I lower them, he tells me to lift them back up and look at him.

"Don't look away," he insists. "Take your pants off and look at me the entire time you're doing it."

This is easier said than done, not only because I find it hard to keep my balance, but also because he has this weird way of piercing me down when he's looking at me. It's intimidating, and oddly sexy.

I step out of my pants and make sure to get rid of my socks as well, even though he never specified for me to do that. Luckily, I'm not wearing the worst underwear in my closet, but I'm sure he's seen way better than the simple black thong that I chose today. This is not my date set of underwear; the bra doesn't even match. Then again, I didn't expect to be on display to anyone like this today.

In any case, he looks pleased. While I sigh in relief when he breaks eye contact, it's quickly replaced by insecurity when his eyes travel along my partly naked body, taking in the sight of my legs and my center. His eyebrows furl when I move my hands to the middle in an attempt to shield myself from his intrusive eyes.

"Good girl," he says. "Now, come."

He beckons me to sit down on his lap like he asked me to before. I stagger toward him, carefully straddling him while placing my hands on the backrest of the love seat sofa. I'm awkwardly sitting on his thighs, but he won't have it and instantly grabs my butt to pull me closer, forcing my throbbing center right on top of his crotch. I gasp in surprise and pleasure.

He's hard already. I can feel his steel rod pushing against my entrance, teasing me through way too many layers of fabric.

"That's better," he says, pulling me in for a kiss. He leaves one hand on my behind, groping me while his other hand takes control of my head by grabbing a fistful of hair and pushing me in even closer, while his tongue invades my mouth.

I moan and let it happen. His touch is so gentle, yet so demanding at the same time. No man has ever touched me like this, so perfectly balanced. I'm breathless during our kiss, giving into his domineering demeanor. It doesn't take long for me to follow up with my own signal of need, and I start grinding on his lap, deliberately teasing his hardness. My heart jumps when I can feel him getting even harder beneath me.

But just as I intend to lift my hands from the backrest to touch him, he stops me again by pushing my arms back down before his right hand is back on the side of my waist, slowly tracing along the hem of my thong.

"Are you wet for me?" he asks, breaking our kiss while his brown eyes stare into me.

I blush at the question, biting my lower lip instead of giving him a reply.

"Shall I find out myself?" he adds, and before I'm capable of coming up with any kind of reply, he skillfully moves my thong aside and dips his fingertips between my hot lips.

I inhale audibly, filled with arousal and shame as his finger slides along my slick entrance. He portrays a winner's smile and nods.

"You're dripping," he states the obvious. "And we haven't even started yet."

My face is smoldering hot, and I'm sure he can see the fiery color of shame written all over me. I don't understand this. He's right, we've only been kissing. But with him, it's not just the physical acts that feed my excitement. It's the way he looks at me, the way he talks to me, the way he orders me around.

"Let me make this easier for you," he says, and before I can ask what he means by that, he adds another finger to have his way between my legs. He caresses my wetness, while making sure that I don't break eye contact by holding my head in place with his other hand. I want nothing more than to look away, avert my eyes, close them, hide away the shame that comes with this new kind of arousal.

What is he doing to me?

"I want you to come," he hisses an answer to my unspoken question.

I shake my head. "No, not y —"

"Yes," he interrupts. "You need a release. Now."

I don't want this to end so soon, but he's not giving me a choice. I'm already so close to coming that I don't doubt his imminent success, but I still try to fight it.

Of course, he notices and intensifies pressure on my sensitive spot. I yelp with pleasure when he starts to draw circles around my swollen clit while fingering me simultaneously.

"Please, n —"

"Yes!" he interrupts, adding another finger and increasing the pressure on my swollen and sensitive nub. I find myself grinding on his hand, desperate for release and stubborn not to follow his wish at the same time. I close my eyes, and to my surprise, he lets me do so. Screw this. I decide to surrender to his demand, throwing my head back while moving my hips in circling motions to get the best out of his talented fingers.

"Good girl," he praises my efforts. "Come."

Hearing his voice, saying that word in his trademark husky tone, adds to my bliss. I've never had that happen before. His voice seems to have almost as much of an effect on me as his hands.

My climax is imminent, approaching in shy waves that grow into a wild storm. I open my eyes when the first wave big enough to steal my breath takes over me - and am met with his triumphant smile as my muscles clench around his fingers. I groan helplessly as wave after wave jerks my body into a defenseless tremor.

He leaves his hand between my legs, waiting for me to ride all the way to the end of my orgasm, before he withdraws his fingers from inside of me.

I've been breaking a sweat and now that my climax is receding, the sheer bliss of it is quickly replaced by an odd sense of confusion and remorse.

But I feel relaxed, and catch myself leaning on his shoulder, placing an intimate kiss on his neck as if we've been lovers for a long time.

That's what it feels like. He's basically a stranger to me, but nothing about him feels like it.

He lets me rest on his shoulder, finally moving his hand out of my lap and - to my horror - licking his fingers clean before he wraps his arms around me. I stiffen in his embrace, once again burning with embarrassment. Did he really just do that?

"Delicious," he comments, as if he's reading my mind.

I bury myself in his embrace, grateful for the fact that he doesn't make me look at him right now. It would be too much.

"I'm not done with you," he whispers in my ear.

"I know," I reply. Neither am I. I want more of this. More of him.

He grabs me by the shoulders and pushes me backward enough so that we can face each other. My thong is still pulled to the side, exposing myself in the most inappropriate fashion, but I suppress the urge to correct it. I have a feeling he would not like that at all.

Kingston looks at me, handsome as ever, while I don't even want to imagine what I must look like. My hair is undoubtedly a mess, I'm sweating, and what little makeup I put on this morning must be smeared by now.

He doesn't seem to care one bit. He still looks at me as if I was the most beautiful woman on the planet. I don't know how he does it, how he can hold this intense level of eye contact for so long, how he can stare at someone with this kind of intensity.

I lower my eyes, only to be met with his finger below my chin.

"Why do you always try to escape this?" he asks, gently lifting my chin up so I'm forced to look him in the eyes.

"I'm not," I object. "It's just... odd."

He smiles. "I enjoy looking at you. Why is that odd?"

"Oh, come on! Me?" I exclaim. "You must've had so much prettier women."

He furls his eyebrows, his eyes filled with a dark promise, and before I know it, his hands are attacking the buttons of my blouse.

"What have I told you?" he asks. His voice is stern and deep, there's nothing playful about the way he speaks.

I look at him, biting my lower lip. I know he told me not to mention any other women while I'm with him, but I couldn't help it. What woman doesn't compare herself to others, especially when faced with a man like him?

He starts unbuttoning my blouse, repeating his question. "What have I told you?"

"No mentioning other women," I whisper. My pulse speeds up with every button he unhooks.

"And what did you just do?" he asks, after he's undone with the last button.

I look at him, narrowing my eyes. What's happening right now?

"What do you m –"

"Didn't you just do that?" he asks, interrupting me. He looks at me with a sinister face, while his hands trace up along my torso, below the unbuttoned blouse, tickling my exposed skin. I shudder and try to suppress a giggle.

"Didn't you just mention other women?" he asks. "Didn't you just do something I told you not to do?"

My eyes widen with incomprehension while his hands travel up to my shoulders, taking the blouse with him. He takes it off, letting the thin fabric slide down my arms, so that I end up sitting on his lap, wearing nothing but my underwear.

"Elodie?" he presses, still looking at me as if I've done something very, very bad.

Maybe I have. I didn't follow his clearly stated rules.

And he warned me.

There'd be punishment.

CHAPTER XIX

Kingston

Elodie is such a good girl, so careful and shy. I almost feared she wouldn't give me any reason to punish her when I needed one. But then she let her insecurity get the better of her and there it was.

Her type of beauty is not easy to find, and she devalues herself and me by comparing herself to the silly bimbos I can pick up at a nightclub any time. I hate when she does that, that's why I imposed that rule - and I knew she'd break it at some point.

Elodie doesn't say a word or make a move when I take off her blouse, but she lets out a faint sigh when I unhook her bra and set her perky breasts free. She sits exposed in front of me, straddling me with her cute little thong still pushed to the side so that I can see her naked lips.

"So, you're not going to answer me," I state, cupping her breasts without any disturbing fabric inhibiting my touch for the very first time.

She looks at me as if she's trying to solve a puzzle, while leaning into my touch at the same time. I pinch her nipples, causing her to yelp in surprise and returning her focus to me instead of whatever was going on inside that pretty head.

"Come here," I whisper, pinching her sensitive nipples and pulling her closer for a kiss.

She gasps in pain and her hands jerk up in an attempt to protect herself, but I push them aside with my arms, without letting go of her nipples. I intensify the pressure, twisting and turning her hard nubs between my fingers while our tongues intertwine, underlined with the sweet sound of her anguished moans. Her moans are a mixture of pain and arousal. Perfect.

I need to be inside her.

My hands let go of her tortured nipples and trail along her ribs, to the side, following the curve of her slim waist down to her ass. She leans into me, not only welcoming my kiss, but heating it with hungry bites. She lifts herself up and rubs her partly exposed legs on my hard cock, begging for it like a good girl.

"Take me out," I breathe between our kisses.

She lets out a desperate sigh and reaches for my crotch, clumsily fiddling with my belt and zipper before she pulls the hindering material aside and closes her talented fingers around my erection. I've been waiting so long for this that the sensation of her touch is almost too much to bear. She starts stroking my length while moving her hips in a way that drives me insane.

I know myself and I know how fast things can get out of hand once I set my mind on something, which is why I'm always carrying protection with me. I reach inside the inside pocket of my suit jacket and produce a condom. All the while, my lips never leave hers. She groans when she hears the plastic ripping and moves her hand aside so that I can roll the condom over my impatient cock. I'm practiced at this, but my hands still tremble as the overwhelming need for her takes over my senses.

She wraps her hand around my length while I push her soaked panties farther to the side. We moan in unison when my tip finally teases her wet entrance. I didn't plan for it to happen like this, but my desire for her got the better of me. She's trying to take the lead, but I don't let her. When I beckon her to lower herself onto my hardness, she moves her hand aside and I take it, grabbing a hold of both her hands and forcing them behind her back while pulling her down onto me. She throws her head back, her eyes closed and her mouth partly opened in that seductive manner I've come to adore so much.

A hearty groan escapes her delicate lips as my cock stretches her. Despite my torturous need for her, I manage to control myself enough to maintain a slow pace, watching as she enjoys every single inch gliding inside her. When I'm all the way in, I keep her pushed down on my lap for a few moments, observing her raw reactions as she moans and squirms on my lap.

"Ride me," I tell her. "Ride that cock, Elodie."

Her eyes flicker open and she looks at me with an expression of dazed lust. I move her hands to the front, letting them rest on my shoulders because I know this will make it easier for her.

She leans forward, her face dangerously close to mine as she lifts herself up and starts riding me just like I told her to.

I don't kiss while I fuck. For me, kissing is just a way of convincing a girl to follow me into the bedroom, but once she's there, naked and with her legs spread in front of me, I have no further need or desire for kissing.

With Elodie, it's different. I want to lock my lips onto hers while she's riding my manhood, claiming her with everything I have, getting closer to her...

Instead of leaning backwards and thrusting my hips up to fuck her, I find myself leaning forward, closer to her beautiful face, drawn to that exotic expression of hers. She doesn't look like she did while playing the piano. This is not the face of a virtuoso musician in her element, but the face of a beautiful girl losing her carefully built facade in passion.

It's so fucking endearing.

I can feel her ecstatic breath on my face.

I can't take this anymore. This face. She's driving me mad. Kissing while fucking? Who the hell am I?

She's closing her eyes, ready for me to kiss her, but just before our lips meet, I jump up from my seat, taking her with me. I grab her by the ass, my cock still planted inside her while I'm standing up, giving her a few more thrusts as if I wanted to fuck those silly thoughts away. She stares at me through wide eyes, startled by my sudden motion.

I decide that I can no longer look at this face if I want to stay true to who I am and toss her on the sofa.

"Turn around," I hiss. "Face the window, show me that ass."

She obeys immediately, placing her hands on the backrest of the sofa and facing the city below while hollowing her back for me. This is it, this is how she's supposed to be fucked by me.

I don't waste another moment before shoving myself back inside of her, causing her to yelp with pleasure. She wants to turn around and look at me, but I stop her from doing so by grabbing her hair and pinning her down with her face straight ahead. No more seductive looks. She'll face the city while I fuck her into oblivion.

I know I won't last long. My release is dangerously close, but I have to make sure that she'll join me. Her tight pussy is clenching around me, hungry for my cock and taking every thrust like a good girl. But I've fucked enough women in my life to know that most of them need more than this to reach their climax, and this is a good moment to find out what this girl needs. I raise my hand, ready to explore Elodie's needs.

She yelps when I slap her behind, and instantly she dips her back even more. Another slap and she moans, pushing her hips backward and inviting me in even further. My hands land on her firm ass for a third time, providing more evidence that she's into this.

Good, very good.

I give her a few more slaps, every single one more intense than the one before, and her moans become louder and more desperate. I know she's close, and I want to send her over the edge.

"Come," I tell her as I reach between her legs, finding her swollen clit. "Come for me."

I don't have to play with her sensitive nub very long before I feel her muscles tightening around me. Elodie's moans come from deep inside her, filling the room while I grab her hips with both hands, ready to join in her release and follow her over the edge.

The sound of her blissful screams eggs me on so much that I come within moments, my voice joining hers as I come deep inside of her.

CHAPTER XX

Elodie

There it is again, that feeling of remorse. It's happened in my life before, when I've regretted sleeping with someone, but it was usually because the sex was so unfulfilling that I might as well have spent the time practicing, or sleeping for that matter. I never get enough sleep, and it often struck me as stupid to waste the extra hours I could have been sleeping on some random guy's dick.

Then again, I'm only human and I have needs. That's what makes me do it again and again.

That's what made me do this. My stupid lust has seduced me to do something so dangerously dumb that I'm almost afraid of myself. I can't believe I'm here, in my client's apartment, freshly fucked by a man who's about to get married to another woman.

However, my remorse has nothing to do with sexual disappointment this time. Not at all. On the contrary. I'm still disoriented and shivering in the aftermath of what just happened.

He didn't want me to get dressed right away, and gave me a soft robe to wear instead. It's one of his bathrobes and way too big for me, hanging loose across my narrow shoulders with the tips of my fingers barely peaking out when I have the sleeves all the way down. It's the softest material I've had covering my naked skin and it smells of him. The fact that I'm naked underneath it is a constant reminder of our adventure, and a promise for more.

"You haven't said a word," he growls next to me.

We are sitting on the sofa opposite the one where he just fucked me, facing the nocturnal city skyline outside. He turned off all the lights and only lit two candles on the table in front of us, which not only bathes the room in a somber light, but also allows for a better view outside the window. The view is breathtaking and has occupied me for minutes, as I've tried to cope with the events of tonight. He's poured me another glass of the best champagne I'll ever drink in my entire life, and I savor every drop of it. This night is almost over and I dread it coming to an end.

I don't want to go, but I know I'll have to. And I know I can't come back.

"I'm just… exhausted," I whisper, turning to him. It's so dark that I can barely see his face, even though he's curled up right next to me. But as far as I can tell, he's smiling.

"Why are you getting married to a woman you don't love?" I ask the question that's been at the back of my mind the entire time.

He sighs. "I told you, it's complicated."

"Are you saying I'm too stupid to understand?" I ask.

He shakes his head. "I would never call you stupid."

"Then tell me," I say. "I want to understand this. After all, I'm involved in it."

He chuckles.

"Professionally, I mean!" I add. "I'm hired for a fake wedding, don't I deserve to know what it's all about?"

"I don't know about that, but I'll tell you nonetheless," he says. "As you know, my family owns one of the biggest shipping companies in this country."

I nod. "Of course, I know that."

"Well, while my grandfather made a fortune with it during his time as the CEO, after my father took over, things kind of went downhill," he explains. "Like a lot of big businesses, our company is slow to adapt to change and new technologies. But it's been made all the worse by my father's inability to comprehend the changes that are taking place without him."

Kingston pauses, absentmindedly caressing my arm. Even after what we just did, his touch still feels surreal to me.

"Accounting, container handling - a lot of those things are still done like they were decades ago," he continues. "It's slowing down productivity and it causes too many errors. We're losing clients left and right because of it. But my father is just stuck in his old ways and won't listen to me. He's so fucking stubborn and set on the idea that he can only hand over the business to a real man. So far, neither me nor my brother qualify for that."

"You have a brother?" I ask randomly.

"Yes, he's younger than me," Kingston says. "Younger and worse than I ever was. He fled to the West Coast when he started college, and never came back. It's easy for him because he doesn't care. He doesn't need to care because I'm the first-born. I need to become the 'real man' my father is waiting for."

"And a real man is... married?" I ask.

Kingston sighed. "Yes. Settled, safe and sane. Married. Married to the right woman."

"That's so..."

"Fucked up?" he completes my sentence.

"I was going for old-fashioned, but yeah, that, too."

"It is," he says. "But if it's what I have to do, I'll do it."

"And Gloria?" I ask. "She's the right woman, because...?"

"Because her parents want her to get married as much as my father wants me to," he replies. "And because she has as little interest in love and marriage as I do. It's the only thing we have in common. We can tie the knot for our parents' sake, and then leave each other alone."

"You don't believe in love?" I ask. "What does that even mean?"

Kingston looks at me. Even in the dark, I can see him furling his eyebrows.

"I don't do love," he says. "That better?"

I shake my head. "No. You just don't know what you're talking about."

"Don't get cocky with me," he warns. "And don't think you can prove me wrong."

His words create an uncomfortable pinch on my heart. I don't know if it's because I feel hurt at this reminder of the nature of our relationship, or because he insinuates that I could be stupid enough to think that I'm the magic princess who can turn him around. Of course, I don't believe that. I'm baffled enough at the fact that he showed any interest in me at all.

"Don't worry, I'll go home soon," I tell him.

"Who says you have to?" he asks.

"Well, you kinda' did. And I do," I insist. "I have class early in the morning."

He snorts. "What a lame excuse."

I frown at him, but know that he can't see it.

"It's not," I object. "This is going to be my job, and I can't miss class if I want to make it in the real world."

"Is that so?" he asks, leaning closer so that I can see the creases in his handsome face as he smirks at me. "What a good girl you are."

"I'm a poor girl first and foremost," I say. "I simply can't afford to fail a class or show any kind of neglect in my studies because I could lose my scholarship if I do."

That's exaggerating a little, but I somehow feel the urge to remind him that we live in very different worlds. His world of wealth and hedonistic activities may be the only one he knows, but my reality is a lot harsher than that. I've always been careful about not missing a single class, getting as much practice in as possible, and leaving a good impression at my part-time job, even if it meant my free time and any kind of socializing would suffer because of it.

"No worries," he says. "I have no intention on keeping you here all night. I don't do that."

Even though his words go along with what I just said, they still leave a painful sting in my heart.

"Oh, another thing you 'don't do'. How rigorous," I mock him.

"I'll call a car to take you home," he adds, ignoring my remark. "But let's finish that champagne first."

I won't argue with that, and take another sip of the wonderful golden liquid. It would be nice to be part of his world, just to have this marvelous drink whenever I craved it.

"You enjoyed yourself," he says. It's not a question, but a statement of confidence.

"Yes," I admit. "That was fun."

He looks at me, and even in the dark I can tell that he's raising an eyebrow at me.

"That was fun," he repeats, mimicking my voice. "One could think I'd taken you to a fair and bought you some sweets instead of making you come so hard you almost passed out. Twice."

I blush and bring the glass up to my lips.

"It was a nice momentary escape," I whisper. "Better than any I've had before."

"Escape from what?" he wants to know.

I pause for a moment, my eyes resting on the beautiful urban night view.

"Life," I say. "Reality."

"This is not part of life?" he asks, sounding indignant. "Am I not real?"

"You know what I mean," I say, casting him a quick look from the side. "Call it normalcy or everyday world if you will."

"Tell me what that looks like," he probes. "Your everyday life."

"Why?"

He chuckles and - to my surprise - wraps his arm around me. Unlike me, he's still fully dressed, which strikes me as odd. I've never had sex without the guy ending up just as naked as I was. It's a shame I will never get to see his - what I expect to be gorgeous - body.

"I can fuck you, but I can't have a conversation with you?" he asks, squeezing me close to him.

"You don't have to fake interest in me," I whisper.

"Don't be so stubborn."

His voice has changed. He sounds genuinely annoyed now.

"Fine," I say. "I wake up, I usually have classes in the morning, sometimes I work at my part-time job during lunch hour, but it's mostly in the afternoons or evenings, and I have private lessons, and then time that I use to practice by myself."

I look at him. "Boring, isn't it?"

"Not to me," he says. "What kind of classes do you have?"

I sigh. "Music Theory, Music History, Piano Performance, Electives. Stuff like that."

"What's your favorite?"

"Anything that lets me play," I quickly reply, causing him to chuckle. "I'm not a theory girl."

"You're very talented," he says, again giving me that weird squeeze.

"Don't take this the wrong way," I say. "But how would you know? You've only heard me a few times, and I reckon you know very little about music, and piano performance specifically."

"Maybe," he admits. "But I did have some lessons myself. When you grow up in a family like mine, it's a must."

"Yes, your mother mentioned that. Lucky bastard," I whisper. "I would have killed for that."

"For what?"

"For growing up in an environment that enforces musical education," I say, hiding behind my glass again. "I was always the oddball with my interest in the piano."

His eyes are on me, and even in the dark his gaze doesn't fail to intimidate me with its intensity. This man confuses me. If all the stories I've heard about him are true, his current behavior does not fit it at all. Why would he put his arm around me like that? Why would he ask me to stay to talk? Why is he feigning this interest in me when it's clear this was all about carnal lust and nothing more?

"When did you start to play?" he wants to know.

I shrug. "Hard to say. I remember my dad taking me to one of his friends' places when I was about five or six. They had a piano and I was drawn to it instantly. I played around with it a little bit, and while my father kept pulling me away and apologizing for the disturbance I caused, his friend's wife encouraged me. She was a musical teacher at an elementary school. She was the one who made it possible for me to have lessons because we could never have afforded it."

"And your mother?" he asks.

My chest tightens. "She's dead."

That's a lie. I never buried my mother. As far as I know, she could still be alive, but I haven't seen her in more than twenty years. She left my father because of his heavy drinking, and never bothered to take me with her. She may have started a new life God knows where, but she's certainly dead to me.

Kingston clears his throat and shifts around uncomfortably. "I'm sorry."

"It's okay," I assure him. "It was a long time ago."

"Mmhmm," he mumbles, his dismay is palpable.

We sit in silence for a few moments, and then he refills our glasses, emptying the bottle. My tolerance for alcohol is surprisingly low, considering that it's been a constant companion on the weekends when I allowed myself to let loose. It's the only outlet I've had to deal with the stress and burden of my aspirations, and I've always worried that I might have inherited my father's dangerous tendencies in this area.

Maybe it's because of the champagne, maybe it's because of Kingston's soothing company, but I feel dizzy and tired, more than I'd expected I would after a few glasses of champagne.

I need to go home. As hard as it is to leave this place, I need to go. I'm getting too comfortable.

"I should go," I give voice to my thoughts.

Kingston takes another sip from his glass and nods. "Yes, you should."

I don't know why it hurts when he's agreeing with me, but the sting is undeniable. I don't want to stay - but I want him to want me to stay. How ridiculous.

Kingston places his glass on the coffee table and turns to me, his arm wrapped around me, while his other hand travels below the robe, tracing along the skin of my thigh. I shiver with desire, but shake my head at the same time. "No."

He chuckles, and when he leans in to kiss me, I almost lose it. His lips meet mine with unaccustomed softness, while he holds me in his loving embrace. He breaks our kiss and looks me in the eyes with calm determination.

"When can I see you again?" he asks.

CHAPTER XXI

Kingston

Sitting through these damn family dinners filled with jabbering about wedding preparations has become even more insufferable than ever before. My betrothed, Gloria, is sitting next to me, faking interest in flowers and centerpieces. I'm beginning to feel that she's decided to take advantage of the situation as much as she can. After all, weddings are all about the bride. That makes it easier for me to keep to the sidelines, but it also provides her with a stage for her narcissism. It's disgusting.

"Only three weeks," she pipes, casting me a look from the side. "Aren't you excited?"

Three weeks until the engagement party. The planning for that unnecessary event is almost concluded, so now the women have moved on to the actual wedding, and while the excitement is growing all around me, I feel as if someone is slowly but steadily choking me to death.

Elodie wasn't supposed to happen. Not like this.

I was supposed to be done with her after three fucks at the most. That's how it works. Instead, I find myself agonizing about the fact that I can't claim her whenever I want to. She said she knew all about me, and she didn't expect anything more than a one-night stand. That's why she just gave me a confused stare when I asked her when I could her again after our first night together.

"Why would you?" was her first response.

And she's right. We should have left it at that. I've been careful about my exploits since it became known that I was to marry the infamous Gloria Waldorf, and fucking the cute little pianist who's supposed to play at our engagement and our wedding reception is anything but smart. I know that, but I can't help it.

Elodie didn't have to tell me how worried she is about her career. I'm not an idiot. But when she tried to refuse to see me again, I had to haul out the big guns. She was still in my apartment, sitting next to me practically naked and buzzed. Some would call it taking advantage, but I didn't fuck her. I just reminded her that I might be the best release she could possibly find to escape from her stressful life. Another orgasm, clenching and squirming around my fingers, and the argument was forgotten.

Still, I've only seen her twice since then. Three times in total, and I'm anything but done with this girl. She's shielded and careful, and asks very few questions about me. We never see each other for more than two or three hours, and I haven't been at my parents' house when she's practicing ever again. I always have a car to bring her directly to my place, and every time I greet her in the driveway, she casts those worried looks toward the guys working at the reception desk downstairs, wondering if it wouldn't be smarter for me to wait for her upstairs. Maybe. But I don't want her to be delivered to me like Chinese food. Sometimes I don't want to be smart, but add a little levity to my life. That's who I am.

Elodie might be the smarter one between the two of us, but she's also the weaker one. I know I can have her as long as I want her.

Trouble is, I don't want to want her this much. This is fucked up. It messes with everything.

"Yes, why would I not be excited," I answer my fiancée's question.

Gloria casts me a suspicious look and then turns her attention back to the food on her plate. It's not like she's going to finish more than half of it. She's a terribly picky eater and avoids every food that could make her fat or look bloated. Of course, the dangerous foods to avoid change every few weeks, always depending on the latest magazine she's consulted.

"That piano girl, is she still coming here to practice?" Gloria asks my mother, catching my attention. Something about the way she's emphasizing her words alarms me, and it doesn't help that she casts another glare in my direction.

"Oh, yes," my mother says from the other end of the table. "She's very diligent. I think she must spend every free minute she has on that piano. Wally told me she usually plays nonstop when she's here. It's been good for her."

"How nice," Gloria says, without meaning it. "But I'm sure she doesn't spend every free minute she has on that piano."

She winks at me and I almost choke on my food as my throat tightens. Everybody at the table saw that weird gesture in my direction. If Gloria is trying to threaten me, I have to admit that she's successful in this moment. But how on earth would she know.

"What do you mean, dear?" my oblivious mother wants to know.

"Oh, nothing," Gloria says innocently. "Just saying. She's a young girl, she'll have other things on her plate, too."

My parents both shrug in unison. My father occupies himself by filling my mother's glass with some more red wine.

"As long as she's doing a good job for us, that's none of our concern," he says.

"Of course," Gloria agrees. "That's all we want from her, right, Kingston?"

That fucking bitch. I give her a glare that should make cocksure what I think of her behavior.

Of course, I can't confront her about it until we're done with dinner and my parents are out of earshot. I'm filled with impatient rage the entire evening, growling my way through bothersome conversation and trying to hide my anger at Gloria. When we're finally calling it a night, Gloria tries to leave the house before me, heading for her car and hoping to reach it before I can reach her. She may think that I won't have the audacity to start an argument in my parents' driveway, but she couldn't be more wrong.

"Hold on!" I bark at her as soon as the front door is closed behind me.

Gloria stops mid-pace and turns around to me, her snake-like eyes opened wide, feigning innocence. "Yes?"

"Give us a minute," I tell her driver, who's holding the car door open for her.

I grab Gloria by the upper arm and lead her around to the other side of the house, out of earshot of both of our drivers. She resists my violent touch and tries to break free, but stands no chance against me. When I let go of her, she dramatically rubs her upper arm and hisses at me, "What the fuck, Kingston! What —"

"Shut up," I interrupt her, my voice harsh but hushed, because I want to make sure that this conversation stays between us. "What was that all about tonight? Why those weird remarks about the piano girl? What were you trying to insinuate?"

Gloria's painted face is illuminated by an oddly bright lantern right next to us, so I can see the grimace she's pulling all too clearly.

"Oh, for God's sake, Kingston, I told you I'm not stupid," she steams. "But you seem to be. You're fucking her, aren't you? The little nerd who's supposed to provide the music at our engagement party."

It's hard to tell whether Gloria sounds hurt or annoyed. Knowing her, I'd assume it's the latter, but she tries to appear hurt for some reason.

"What makes you think that?" I ask.

She rolls her eyes and huffs.

"Please, Kingston. You don't think I talk to Glen once in a while?" she asks. "He keeps me posted on your little exploits, and he's been telling me that she was at your place at least three times now. Isn't that where you draw the line? Fucking three times? You're done now, right?"

I glare at her, boiling with fury. It never occurred to me that she could have any connection to Glen. He has been working for me for years. I trusted that guy!

"Why the hell do you care?" I ask her, instead of reacting to her accusations. "Why the fuck is this any of your business."

She frowns at me.

"I'm your fucking fiancée, you idiot. Of course, this is my business," she says. "I mean, it's one thing if you run around fucking the occasional bimbo, changing your little fuck toys like towels. But *her*? And you're being so careless about it, too! Do you want our parents to find out? You're risking everything with this! She's going to be at our engagement party and our wedding! She's fucking part of it! If word gets out that she's your mistress, what kind of light does that shed on me?"

Her furious eyes blaze up at me.

"She's not my mistress," I object. "You know my rules."

"Well," Gloria says, her eyes flickering. "Does that mean you're done with her? You'd better be."

I look at her, weighing my options. I'm not done with Elodie, but as much as I hate Gloria, she's right in this matter. We both made a pact for this. We agreed to get married so that I could secure my future and save my family's empire from ruin, while Gloria could get her parents off of her back and continue her hedonistic lifestyle while pretending to be my stay-at-home wife and the pretty trophy wife that clings to my arm at formal receptions and festivities. Also, my family's wealth may trump that of hers, so for her this is a financial and social class ascent.

Both our parents have been on our case to get settled down and neither of us has any interest in doing so. That's the only thing her and I have in common, though I would argue that my reasons to agree to this mess has more validity. She just wants to continue to be a party girl, while I want to take the place that's rightfully mine and turn around the mistakes my father and his unworldly associates have implemented. The shipping industry is vastly changing, but he's not adapting to it at all. If I don't take over as soon as possible, our companies may take big hits, endangering everything my grandfather worked for. I've tried to reason with him for years, but he argues that I'm not to be taken seriously unless I'm settled down as a true patriarch.

How fucking backwards. I have a degree, plenty of experience because I've been working at our business for years now, and an entrepreneurial spirit that he and his old buddies lack. But no, I have to put a ring on some pre-selected princess for him to hear me out.

And that alleged princess is now standing before me, her fake lashes fluttering furiously as she awaits my reply.

"Don't worry about it," I tell her. "I have no interest in putting our arrangement in danger."

Gloria looks at me, a sudden somberness traveling across her face.

"You need to remember, Kingston, this deal comes with sacrifices," she says. "We can't have it all, and we can't always have what we want."

I regard her with a skeptical gaze. "What are you talking about?"

"Nothing," Gloria hurries to say, then raising an eyebrow. "Let me just put it this way, Kingston. If you don't stop fucking that girl, I'll make sure she gets replaced. I can't have this kind of risk involved in our little act."

I shake my head, looking at her through narrow eyes. "Are you threatening me?"

Gloria's expression changes into a condescending smirk, the ugliest of faces.

"I'm not threatening you, dear Kingston," she whispers. "I'm just telling you what I'll deem necessary if this doesn't stop. Understood?"

That fucking bitch. I clench my fists and remind myself never to hurt a woman in anger. If this was a play session, I'd bend her over and spank the living hell out of her before reminding her of her place by ramming my cock inside her tight pussy.

But this is not what's happening. She's not a playmate trying to tease me, but an actual bitch who's just pissing me off to no end.

Understood? No one has the right to speak to me like this. No one.

I don't deign her with a reply, but turn around and move toward my car with wide and angry strides.

CHAPTER XXII

Elodie

"I have a surprise for you," he says, as we're riding the elevator up to his place.

He looks at me with a boyish smile, the face of someone who can't wait to see the reaction of a person he's about to present with something special and unexpected.

"A surprise?" I ask, getting closer to him. "What is it?"

"Wouldn't be a surprise if I told you now, would it?" he replies. "Just wait a few more moments. But you'll have to wear this."

He produces a blindfold from the inside pocket of his suit jacket.

"Oh," I say. "Alright."

He puts the blindfold on me just in time, as the elevator reaches its destination on the uppermost floor. I hear the doors open, but don't move until he takes me by the arm and leads me inside his apartment. I've been here before, but my steps are still careful and shy as he gently pushes me inside the living room area. He positions me, turning me slightly to the left.

It's still light outside and I can feel the warmth of the sun shining through the panoramic windows blanketing my skin.

"Ready?" he whispers into my ear, and I nod.

My heart is racing with excitement. I have no idea what to expect.

When he removes the blindfold, I'm instantly blinded by the glaring sun and have to lift my hand to throw a shadow over my face.

Then I see it. In the far left corner of his living room, opposite the seating area we've played on before, there's a brand new Steinway Model D grand piano, standing right beneath the window.

He places his hands on my shoulders, standing at my back as he awaits my reaction.

"Oh my God..." I breathe, trying to grasp what this means. This can't be.

"This... this wasn't here before," I utter helplessly.

Kingston chuckles behind me. "No, it wasn't. Do you like it?"

"Like it?!" I exclaim, turning around to face him. "You did not buy a freaking Model D grand piano for... for me?"

"Well," he says, raising one eyebrow as he cocks his head to the side. "It's in my home. But yes, it's for you to play on."

"But... but," I stutter. "I can't... why did you –"

"So I could watch you play," he says, smirking at me. "Naked, if possible."

I stare up at him in disbelief. "W-w-what?"

"Consider this a present for myself just as much as for you," he explains. "I enjoy watching you play. When I saw you at my parents' place, it did provoke quite a few images. Things I'd like to see."

He leans closer, caressing the outline of my jaw with the tip of his finger as he suggests a kiss, our lips barely touching.

"Things I'd like to do to you while you play," he whispers. "And now, I can."

I shiver with excitement, leaning in to his kiss, only to have him withdraw from me.

"Play," he says, nodding toward the piano. "Play something for me."

"Uh," I mumble, hesitantly turning around to face the beautiful instrument. "Sure."

I approach the grand piano with slow and careful steps, as if I was afraid that I could scare it away. It's the same model that I've played on so many times at his parents' home, but this one is brand new.

"Has it ever been played before?" I ask, as my hand travels along the frame.

"Not that I know of," he says. "I certainly haven't."

I turn around, my hand resting on the fall board. It's not even lifted up.

"But you told me you took lessons as a kid," I say. "I'm sure you could play something."

Kingston shakes his head, a smile appearing on his handsome face as he comes closer.

"That doesn't mean I want to," he says. "I enjoy watching you play way more than doing it myself."

He beckons me to go ahead, and I lift the fall board, exposing the brand new keys underneath. The thought that I'm the first to play this piano is both weirdly frightening and exciting.

"It's as if I'm taking its virginity," I joke, as I sit down on the bench and start adjusting it.

Kingston comes to a halt right next to the piano and casts me a mischievous smile. I know that he's up to something before he opens his mouth to tell me.

"I want you to play naked," he says. "Get up and let me take care of that."

I blush and my heart reacts with a silly hiccup to his demand. My eyes wander up to his, searching for affirmation.

"Get up," he repeats, raising his eyebrows as a warning. "Now."

I do as I'm told, standing next to the bench a moment later. He nods and steps closer, starting to unbutton my blouse right away. His touch is so warm and gentle, but electric at the same time. He must feel my heart racing beneath the few layers of fabric.

"I like that you're wearing a skirt today," he says after removing my blouse and my bra. I'm wearing another ensemble that he sent me a few days ago, an exquisite blouse and a tight-fitting black pencil skirt that ends above my knees. It's a more elegant and more daring outfit than what I'd usually wear, but I put on these clothes especially for him anyway.

He places his hands on my naked shoulders and gently strokes my skin with his thumbs.

"Look at me," he says.

I wasn't even aware that my gaze had lowered again. It's a reflex that's hard to fight, even when he tells me to do it.

As soon as my eyes meet his, he pulls me in for a kiss. He's surprisingly gentle today, not claiming me with the usual force of lust, no biting, no sucking on my lower lip. It would be disappointing if I didn't know that he's restraining himself. I can feel it in his hands, clasping on my shoulders with such power that it almost hurts.

I love his kisses, no matter if they're gentle or demanding. His lips don't move away from mine, while his hands begin to travel down the side of my arms, fondling my skin and causing me to moan with pleasure. I can feel him hook his thumbs beneath the hem of my skirt and into my pantyhose, and flinch in surprise when he pulls them down in one swift motion, taking my panties with him, so that I'm completely exposed.

He breaks our kiss and when I open my eyes to look up at him, I'm met with the unyielding depth of his.

"Don't move," he tells me.

I suggest a nod, my body trembling as he goes down on his knees in front of me, pulling my pantyhose and the skirt all the down to my feet. He nudges me on my ankles and I lift my feet one by one to step out of my clothes. Why am I always the one ending up completely naked before he has taken off even one item of clothing?

His hands trail up along my naked legs, on the outside of my calves until he reaches my knees, and then they move to the inside of my upper thighs.

I yelp when he pinches my sensitive skin, beckoning me to move my feet wider apart, so that he has more leeway.

"Good girl," he comments when I follow his order, exposing myself to him even more.

His face is right in front of my center, and when he reaches up, spreading my lips apart with his thumbs, I can't help but sigh with desperate need, mixed with the heat of shame. This is so weird, and so arousing, at the same time. My eyes drift to the side, fixating on the view, watching as the city bustles below, wondering if anyone can see me from one of the other buildings nearby. I doubt it, because the reflection of the sun on the windows must make it close to impossible to see anything that's going on behind them.

But I can't be certain of that, and for some reason, this uncertainty only adds to my need.

I hold on to the piano when his tongue meets my wet entrance, drawing circles dangerously close to my most sensitive spot, while he hums with approval. No one has ever gone down on me like this, and I'm thoroughly embarrassed by my own arousal.

"You're dripping all over me," he whispers, his mouth still on my lips. "What a naughty girl you are."

I close my eyes, confused by that toxic mixture of yearning and shame.

Kingston gets back up on his feet, causing me to let out a gasp of relief. He raises one eyebrow, smiling as he shakes his head.

"We're only getting started," he announces. "I still want you to play for me, but I will make it a little harder for you."

I search for an explanation in his dark eyes, but instead of giving me one, he finally does something I've been wanting for a long time. He takes a step back and starts taking off his suit jacket, followed by unbuttoning his shirt underneath.

I throw him a thankful smile.

"You'll add a sweet distraction," I presume. "You're right, that won't make it easy."

He shakes his head, but I barely notice because he takes off his shirt in that same moment, exposing his perfectly tanned and toned chest. I've never been one to be seduced by looks alone, but Kingston doesn't just look good. He looks surreal, like a dream come true. His muscles are so defined, they look as if he's an effigy of a Greek god, carved out to perfection.

"Wow," I breathe, incapable of coming up with anything more eloquent to say.

He steps closer, and when I lift my hands to touch him, he grabs me by the wrists, once again taking control, even now. I'm not allowed to touch him of my own will, but he guides my hands along the outline of his broad chest, down to his six-pack and the rifts along his pelvic muscles. I've never seen, let alone touched, a body like his - and I underestimated the effect it would have on me.

"Reach inside my left pants pocket," he tells me, pulling me out of my dazed stream of thoughts.

I look up at him, confused and surprised at this command, but he nods, beckoning me to follow through. I do as he wishes and produce something from his pocket that resembles a bullet, about the size of my thumb. It has a smooth surface texture and is pink with a little string attached to it.

"Do you know what this is?" he asks.

I have a suspicion, but am too shy to say it out loud. My voices fails me, and instead of giving him a proper reply, I just smile up at coyly.

"I want you to wear this," he says, stepping closer and taking the little bullet out of my hands.

He grabs a fistful of my hair and tilts my head back, claiming me with another kiss while his other hand moves back between my legs, parting my lips in one swift move and inserting the bullet inside of me. I'm embarrassed at how easily it slides inside due to my wetness, but he only comments on it with an appreciative hum.

"Play," he breathes, breaking our kiss and letting go of my hair.

I'm trembling and nervous when I sit down on the bench to do something I've done a thousand times before - just not like this.

"What... do you want to hear?" I ask with a trembling voice.

Instead of answering me, I see him reach inside his other pocket, and a moment later, the bullet inside me starts to vibrate, causing me to yelp and flinch in surprise.

"Oh m –"

"Whatever you're thinking of right now," he says, positioning himself next to the piano as he watches me cope with the vibrations inside of me.

"Play."

CHAPTER XXIII

Kingston

Elodie sits on her bench, looking so perfect that I'm inclined to believe that she was made just for me. Her pale skin, her deep brown locks and those exotic green eyes, flickering with nervous lust as she looks at me, the vibrating egg working its magic deep inside of her. I've never seen anything this perfect before, an erotic beauty that's unmatched.

The setting is still on low because I want to give her time to accommodate this undoubtedly strange and new feeling. It has exactly the effect on her that I was hoping for, but she looks so much better than I could have ever imagined.

After I asked her to play for a second time, now with the vibrations torturing her dainty body, she takes in a deep breath, positions herself on the bench and places her fingers on the keys, pausing for another moment before she starts to play her first song. I'm not familiar with the piece she chooses to play, but it sounds different than all the others I've heard before. It's faster and more upbeat than the melancholic and romantic melodies she's been presenting and practicing at my family's home. Even with my untrained ears, I notice that she misses a few notes and speeds up at places where the song is meant to go along at a slower pace. She grimaces every time it happens, visibly disappointed at herself.

But there's one passage that really speaks to her and appears to be so familiar to her talented fingers that even the toy doesn't prevent her from hitting the notes correctly. She sways back and forth in a big circle, closing her eyes as the melody takes her away in perfect sync with the vibrations in her core. It almost looks as if she's about to come, but that better not happen. I didn't give her permission to do so yet.

I slowly move around the piano, painfully aware of the hardness between my legs. I wish I could take a picture of her right now, or capture her beauty in a movie. The sun bathes her fair-skinned body in a warm light as it is about to set, providing the perfect atmosphere for this exclusive performance. Elodie flinches here and there, when the vibrations hit especially sensitive spots. I reach inside my pocket, finding the small remote control and watch as she jumps up in surprise when I turn up the intensity. She groans and adds an unplanned hiccup to the song, but she doesn't stop playing.

"I'm gonna c –"

"No, you're not," I interrupt her, drowned out by the tune she's playing.

I step behind her, placing my hands on her shoulders. She leans back into me, her hands still flying across the keyboard with a professional accuracy that amazes me even now.

My hands trail down on her naked upper body, moving to the front and cupping her perky breasts. I can feel her heart speeding beneath my touch and when I take her nipples between my fingers and squeeze them, she's forced to pause, gasping for air as I torture her cute little nubs.

"Go on," I tell her, without letting go of her.

Her fingers are shaking, but she manages to carry on through the last few notes of the song. She plays the final chord, her upper body now resting in my hands as she leans forward, coping with the sweet pain I'm causing her while the sound of the last and heavy notes fades away.

"Get up," I whisper.

She obeys immediately, her legs shaking when she rises up on her feet.

"Kneel on the bench," I command. "Facing the piano."

She sighs a weak reply, trembling with lust as she positions herself the way I told her to. She's careful not to hit the keyboard, but supports herself on the rim instead, arching her back without me telling her to.

"Good girl," I say, opening my pants with one hand while giving her slap on the ass with the other. She flinches and moans, clearly welcoming it.

The string of the toy is dangling between her legs, drenched with her juices. She enjoyed this even more than I thought she would. I reach inside my pants pocket, producing the remote control and a condom before I let my pants drop to the floor. She sighs when I switch off the toy, and it's hard to tell whether it's of disappointment or relief.

I pull the condom over my hard length and pull on the string, teasing her for a few moments, before pulling the toy out.

"That must have been your best performance yet," I say, putting the toy away. "You need a reward for being such a good girl, don't you?"

She groans with desperate need, hollowing her back and lifting her ass to invite me in. I tease her with the tip of my cock, only pushing the head inside, before I retreat, causing her to moan with frustration.

"Say it," I tell her. "Beg for your reward."

"Fuck me," she breathes. "Please, Kingston. Fuck me."

She looks back at me over her shoulder, her eyes fogged with desire and as beautiful as always.

"I earned it," she whispers.

I smile at her. "That you did."

With those words, I shove my entire length inside of her in one forceful thrust. She welcomes it with a hearty groan, throwing her head back and hollowing her back even further. I wanted to go slow to match the final chords of the song she was playing, but now that I'm inside of her, I can't help it. I need to fuck her. Fast. Hard. Rough. I ram my cock inside of her with brute force, grabbing her by the hip and claiming her with such ferocity that she can barely hold on to the piano. While the sight of her, bent over on the piano bench, her hair falling over her shoulders as she's shaken by my strength, moves me in ways I could never have predicted, it's the image of her playing that really brings me closer to the edge. That elegance, her skillful treatment of this refined instrument, her ethereal beauty while following my wishes.

I can't get enough of it. I can't get enough of her.

So what if I fuck her more than three times? Way more than that.

So what if I keep her?

I'm not letting her go, and I don't care how much trouble this might get me into. She's mine, and I will protect her from any harm that could come from this.

This I swear to myself as I feel my orgasm building up. She's moaning and squirming beneath me, slightly changing the angle by lowering her upper body. I'm just about to give her permission to come, but she defies my orders for once by not waiting for it. I can feel her muscles clenching around my cock when she finds her release, riding the waves of bliss as she comes on my cock like the good girl she is. The perfect girl for me.

I join her ecstasy, letting out a loud groan as I come inside her with one last, long and deep thrust.

CHAPTER XXIV

Elodie

E ven after returning to school, Benjamin managed to avoid me enough to make it impossible for me to confront him about the nasty rumors he's been spreading about me. He can consider himself lucky that I've been this distracted because of my appointment with the Abrams family, and because of Kingston. I don't know what to do about him. I know there's no future for us, but I also can't stay away from him.

He's not making it any easier with his presents and charming messages. He has been sending me more clothes and even jewelry, claiming that I should consider it as an advance, and while I feel uncomfortable about this kind of attention, it also flatters me to no end. Let's be real, what woman wouldn't want a package of well-fitting designer clothing arriving on her doorstep once a week, along with a sweet note? He even picked out some pearl earrings, saying that they would go well with the blouse I wore the night he first fucked me.

And that piano. I still can't believe he bought a model D grand piano for his place just so he could watch me play naked. No one has ever sexualized my talent like he does, and I kind of like it. Not to mention the way he fucked me afterward...

My ears start burning with heat as I remember that evening. It was our best yet, if one was to ask me. Even better than our first night.

My mind has been occupied with him and everything that involves him so much that I find it hard to pay attention to my theory classes, even more so than usual. It also helped in ignoring Benjamin and his disgusting way of dealing with our breakup, if one can even call it that.

That was until I found myself confronted with the rumors he started. It was just a random remark by one of my classmates, a nasty joke that I would have cast aside without thinking about it twice, but given the circumstances, I can't help but wonder if Benjamin is still running around, coping in the worst way possible. So, when I find him sitting by the kitchen table upon my return to our shared apartment, I'm quick to take him to task.

He's all by himself, and by the expression he makes when he sees me entering, I can tell that he's not happy to see me and has no interest in talking to me.

"We need to talk," I say, pointing my finger at him as I approach the kitchen table taking fast steps.

"About?" he asks, trying to appear unfazed, but I can tell that he's nervous.

I sink into a chair opposite him and place my elbows on the table.

"Just one question," I say. "And I want you to answer honestly. Did you, or did you not, tell people that I have sex with others in return for money?"

He frowns at me, but doesn't say a word.

"Did you?" I press. "Did you tell people that I prostitute myself, Benjamin?"

Now, he huffs, shaking his head.

"I don't know why you're so offended," he says. "It's not that far from the truth."

I inhale audibly and shake my head.

"What the hell, Benjamin?" I gasp. "Why would you say something like that?"

"Because," he says, leaning forward and narrowing his eyes. "Because that's what it felt like. I paid for almost everything while we were dating. You took advantage of me and once you found a new sugar daddy, you just dropped me like a toy you're done playing with."

I stare at him in shock. He can't possibly be serious about this.

"You offered to pay every time," I hiss. "I never asked for anything. And besides, what we were doing can hardly be called dating! We had some fun together, that's it. And I'm sorry if you felt like I took advantage of you, but I can assure you, that's not what was going on between us."

I lean back, ruffling my hair in disbelief as I sigh. "I can't believe this."

"Well, next time, maybe you'll think twice before you treat someone else like this," he says, sounding like a stubborn toddler.

"Treat someone else like what?" I ask. "I haven't done anything to you. I've always been honest with you. You, on the other hand, are actively destroying my reputation with these rumors."

Benjamin shakes his head as he gathers up the dishes from the meal he was finishing when I entered.

"Whatever, dude," he says, getting up from his chair and walking over to the kitchen sink.

"Whatever, *dude*?" I repeat, my voice sounding awfully shrill.

Benjamin starts washing his dishes, completely ignoring me. I'm so angry at him, but feel so utterly helpless. He's hurt, rejected. I kind of feel sorry for him, but none of that is an excuse for spreading those awful rumors about me. And it doesn't help that Kingston, my client who I'm sleeping with, is showering me with gifts. I will have to be more careful in this regard. I haven't even told Kim about the gifts, and when she commented on my new wardrobe, I just told her that I got it at some kind of outlet. Kim has never been truly aware of my financial situation, so the fact that I might occasionally shop for designer clothes at outlets should not be anything for her to be suspicious about.

However, Benjamin and his hurt feelings pose a much bigger problem for me. I'm infuriated at his behavior, but I still think it's smarter to take the nice route when attempting to resolve things between us.

"Benjamin, please," I say. "Can't we both be civil about this? I never intended to hurt you, and I'm sorry if there was a misunderstanding between us. But please, stop spreading those nasty rumors about me!"

I get up from the table and walk over to him at the kitchen sink, positioning myself so that I am standing right next to him.

"Please," I repeat.

Benjamin pauses and looks at me. His expression is stern, but I notice that it's only a thin layer of anger hiding a sea of pain.

"Just leave me alone, Elodie," he says, averting his eyes and continuing to wash his dishes, as if it was the most important thing in the world to do.

I don't say another word and escape to my room. Kim isn't here, and if I didn't have to go to work right now, I'd have the luxury of having these four walls all to myself for a while. Between the two of us, she's probably the only one who ever gets to enjoy that luxury because I'm out and about so much.

I leave my backpack and change into my work clothes. Thanks to my pleasant chat with Benjamin, there's no time for anything else, so I head out the door just a few minutes after getting home from my last class. Benjamin is nowhere to be seen and has probably retreated to his own room to chill. I wish I had that kind of luxury.

Then again, I do have Kingston. Kingston, his amazing skills as a lover, and the few evenings I've spent at his wonderful home, drinking champagne that costs almost as much as my monthly rent. I will miss it, once it ends.

We've seen each other enough for me to trust him enough to know that he's not going to threaten my career. Thinking of it now, I don't even understand how I could ever had thought that in the first place. Of course, he doesn't have any interest in our little adventure becoming known to anyone else. We're both interested in secrecy.

A perfect match. A perfect little hookup that can lead nowhere.

Great, isn't it? Just what I always wanted.

I make my way across the hallway, down the stairs, out the door of our building, and over to campus, still trying to shake off the stupid thoughts that try to convince me otherwise.

No, I'm not interested in Kingston Abrams more than I should be.

No, I can't be.

I don't know why he's being so nice to me or why he would invite me to his place again and again, but whatever it is, it can't turn into anything real. Even if there's no love involved, he's going to get married to another woman, and very soon.

I should be worrying about my unfinished playlist for their engagement party more than about our forbidden liaison.

I vow to get him out of my head before my shift at the café starts, but Kingston manages to destroy that resolution by showing up where I least expect him.

He's sitting in one of the chairs in the café, his legs crossed and a tablet in his hand, continuously casting glances at the door, until he sees me. He's not wearing a suit today, but a casual sweater with a shirt underneath, the stiff and milk-white collar a reminder of his bourgeois background. His dark hair is combed to the side, and his strong jaw is sporting perfectly trimmed stubble. No matter where and when I see him, he's the epitome of perfection, even blending in with his environment.

His eyes lock onto me, like they always do when I'm in his proximity, and while this should be a flattering realization, it scares the hell out of me now that he's suddenly appeared in my world.

I pause in the doorway for a moment, staring back at him, and even though it's obvious that he's here to see me, I decide to go on the run and disappear inside the kitchen in the back. It's still early in the afternoon and as quiet as usual. Next to Kingston, there are only a handful of customers, but he's the only one without a drink. I put on my humiliating apron and take a deep breath before I approach his table, trying to look professional, as if I was coming up to him for nothing more than an order.

"What can I do for you?" I ask, keeping my distance and casting nervous looks around. Of course, no one is paying attention to us.

"I needed to see you," he says, completely unfazed by his surroundings.

"Here?" I hiss. "Now? Why? I have to work!"

Kingston looks around, his eyes wandering back and forth between me and the café's interior.

"It doesn't look like the place is very busy right now," he says. "I'm sure you'll have time for a little chat."

He beckons me to sit down next to him, but I hesitate.

"What's this about?" I ask. "Why didn't you just text me?"

"If I tell you that it's about your job, would you sit down for a minute?" he replies back.

My heart skips a beat in fright.

"Why? What's going o –"

"Sit down," he tells me in that same domineering voice he uses when we're alone in his apartment. And I comply, just as I would then.

"Good girl," he whispers, causing me to straighten up with alarm.

"Kingston, please," I breathe. "Not here."

He smirks at me. "But I enjoy seeing you like this."

"What's going on?" I repeat my interrupted question, ignoring his smug look. "Were there any changes? Anything I should know? Are you firing me?"

Kingston smiles, but shakes his head.

"No, nothing like that," he says. "I actually meant this job, here."

He makes a gesture around the room.

"What about it?" I ask.

"I want you to quit it," he says. "I don't want you to waste your time with this when it could be spent with me - and your talent."

"What?!" I hiss at him. "I can't quit my job. I know this may come as a surprise to you, but I don't have a trust fund I could live off of, Mr. Abrams. I can't rely on my family to pay for this, I have no savings, and I haven't relied on my drunkard father's assistance since I was in junior high."

His eyes flicker at that sensitive information I just confessed about my father, and I realize that I've never told him about the full extent of my impoverished upbringing.

"See, that's where you're wrong," he says. "You do have someone to rely on now. Me."

I tilt my head to the side, pursing my lips as I try to grasp where he's going with this.

"You see, Elodie," he says, leaning forward and placing his elbows on the table between us. "I want more of you. And I always get what I want. But I don't want to take away your time at the piano. You need that. I respect your aspirations and I have no intentions of getting in the way of that. Still, I want more of your time. And as I see it, the only time you can spare is the time you'd spend at this useless job."

"It's not useless," I insist. "It pays my bills. I need it."

"No, you don't. Not if I take up paying those bills for you," he says. "You know it's nothing to me, and it would help you in so many ways."

I stare at him with disbelief. Why is he doing this? How can he offer something so outrageous to me? I feel like the universe is trying to play a joke on me. Benjamin accuses me of taking advantage of men and treating them as sugar daddies, and then just a few minutes later, Kingston offers to do just that for me.

"I'm sorry, I can't accept that offer," I tell him.

Kingston furls his eyebrows and sighs.

"Elodie, don't be stupid about this," he says.

"I'm not," I reply, rising from my seat. "In fact, I think that's the first time I'm smart about something in regard to you."

With that, I walk away from the table, confident that his eyes are following me.

CHAPTER XXV

Kingston

It turns out that Gloria's warning had the exact opposite effect of what she intended. Instead of letting go of Elodie, I just want her even more. Forbidden fruits have always tasted the best, and this one is like no other.

My offer to pay for her expenses so that she doesn't have to work at that stupid job anymore is not a purely charitable gesture. It would be another way to bind her to me, make her dependent on me. Own her.

The thought of making her mine in more ways than just fucking her has haunted me since our first encounter. When Gloria called her my mistress, I actually liked it. I like the idea of having her in my life like that. In a twisted way, this would even be more acceptable than what I've been doing before. The tiresome flow of ever-changing but somehow identical beauties I picked up along the way of partying my way through New York

City's elite hedonistic nights was fun for a while, but it's also frowned upon. Hence my father's wish for me to settle down. I know I'm seen as the bad seed in this family, even though I know that my younger brother is no better than me. But he's far away, living his exploits on the West Coast, out of sight and free from any obligation.

Of course, I could never tell a girl like Elodie to be my mistress. That's not how things work for girls like her. All I have is to gradually get her there - and then figure out how to deal with the problem that may arise if she gets too attached. Or if I do.

Thing is, I'm too attached already. It shows in every pathetic action I take toward her. She sent me off like an annoying bard singing below her balcony, and instead of letting it go, I make sure to be around when she ends her shift. I know her schedule because she told me every detail when I asked.

No girl has ever rejected me or anything I have to offer like she just did. I can't let it go, and I won't.

It's after ten o'clock when she finally walks out of the coffee place, completely unaware that I'm watching her from afar. I'm on her heels within a few moments, waiting until we are in a more secluded location before I come up close behind her and grab her by the arm.

Just like any woman who thinks she's about to get attacked, Elodie swirls around, trying to break free from my grip, and then yelping in surprise.

"Kingston!" she gasps, with a solid tone of relief in her voice. "What are you-?"

I interrupt her by pulling her closer and forcing my lips on hers. She squirms and tries to fight me, but her attempts are half-hearted and lead nowhere. It's nothing but a staged show, her mind fighting over her body. Luckily, the latter wins, and soon her wails of protest turn into moans of desire. I pull her closer, wrapping my other arm around her to press her against me, letting her know that there's nowhere else for her to be right now but safe within my demanding embrace.

"Not here," she breathes when I end our kiss. "Not here, we're outside, it's dangerous. People can see..."

I look at her, her face desperate with need and tormented by an internal struggle I only know too well.

"Forbidden pleasures alone are desired immoderately," I whisper.

She looks at me, her eyes wide in bewilderment.

"See, even the old Romans knew about this predicament," I tell her. "They just found better words for it."

Elodie smiles. "Did they play with fire like this, too?"

She surprises me by going up on her toes and planting another quick kiss on my lips.

That little minx. I grab her by the hair, pulling on it so she's forced to tilt her head back. She's grimacing with pain, but doesn't manage to hide the smile that barges in between.

"I need you," I whisper. "Now."

Her eyes flicker. "No. Not here."

"Wrong answer," I tell her, shaking my head. "You know I always get what I want."

I lift my hand and gently caress her cheek. "And if you don't propose an alternative, I'm going to fuck you right here, where anybody could come by and see us, any moment."

She bites her lower lip. "You wouldn't."

"Try me."

A few moments pass, and we remain in that close embrace, staring at each other while our bodies heave with wanton lust. She's so responsive to me, but yet so classy in her yearning.

"Come," she breathes, freeing herself out of my embrace and turning around, beckoning me to follow her. Just as we turn around the corner, there's a small group of students who undoubtedly would have run right into us if we had stayed in that alley and followed up on my threat.

Elodie walks two steps ahead of me, striding at a fast pace while her brown hair flies behind her. I soon realize that she's leading me back to the café where she works. It's past closing time and all the lights are switched off. Elodie produces a key from her purse and unlocks the door, beckoning me to follow her. I step inside and she hurries to lock the door behind us and then closes the blinds.

"So cute," I comment.

She turns around and even through the faint light that the moon casts inside, I can see her bright smile beaming at me.

"It gets better," she whispers, nodding towards something behind me. My eyes follow her gesture and as I turn around, I see a sofa corner in the far back.

"Sofas are your thing, aren't they," she whispers.

It's true, I have never taken her to my bedroom so far, and right now I'm wondering why that is. If anyone belongs in there, it's her.

I turn back to her and lift her up, our lips meeting for another kiss while she wraps her slim legs around my waist as I carry her over to the sofa. I put her on the cushions, on her back, and immediately start to undress her, removing her coat and throwing it on the floor before moving on to the shirt she's wearing underneath. It's a simple long arm shirt, not one of the pieces that I sent to her. I lift it up, exposing her bra underneath, as she moans with desire. I move my hand to her back and unhook it, exposing her perky breasts. She's lying in front of me, her naked chest heaving as the moonlight shines in on her. What a beautiful sight. I lean forward, kneading her breasts with both my hands and sucking on one of her nipples. She's so sensitive, I know this will drive her mad. And it does. Elodie groans with pleasure, arching her back beneath me as she leans into me, begging for more and grinding against my body. I add little bites to my treatment, causing her to yelp in pain, but she doesn't fend me off.

But when she lifts her hands and tries to undress me, I stop her by grabbing her wrists and am met with a disappointed sigh.

"You never let me," she breathes. "I want to see you. Touch you."

I look at her, fighting an internal battle as I ponder why I'm so uncomfortable with this. I've never liked having a girl take charge of me by undressing me and enjoying my body the way I enjoy hers.

But Elodie may deserve it.

"Earn it," I tell her.

"How?" she breathes.

"You know what I want," I say.

Elodie looks up at me, furling her eyebrows as she begins to understand what I'm getting at.

"No," she whispers. "Are you still talking about that?"

"I won't stop talking about it until you agree," I tell her.

She frowns up at me and straightens up, shielding her bare chest from my eyes by pulling her shirt down.

"That will never happen," she says, glaring at me.

"Well, then there are some things you'll have to do without," I tell her.

"Are you trying to blackmail me?" she asks.

I huff, shaking my head. "What an ugly word."

"It's very fitting," she says.

We look at each other, neither of us willing to back down. She's just as stubborn as I am, and her unyielding gaze darkens as she comes to a painful conclusion. She lowers her eyes as her facial expression changes to somber sadness.

"I think you should go," she whispers.

CHAPTER XXVI

Elodie

The funny thing is that it felt good. Putting Kingston Abrams in his place felt good and right. I don't like the way he's trying to gain power over me by practically buying me. It would have been so easy to say yes to his offer, to have a little sugar daddy who's willing to pay me just so I don't work at this tiring job anymore.

But I've never been one to choose the easy way. I'm a hard worker and proud of it. I've been on my own financially since I was a teenager, and it feels good to know that I've earned my way up.

This was the right thing to do.

I've never felt more powerful in my life.

The only thing that bothers me is his silence. I haven't heard from him since that night, not one message. I didn't think rejecting his offer would mean the end of whatever this was between us, but apparently, that's how he took it.

It hurts to think that. I thought I was being rational about this. He was just a dangerous fling, great sex, a few exclusive amenities that I could never afford on my own, a sweet little release from my hard-working world. He wasn't supposed to be anything more.

But I've fallen for the way he looks at me, the way his eyes cling to me when I speak, this sincere interest he appears to have in me.

Also, let's face it. This wasn't just great sex. It was the best sex I've ever had. He was also the best company I've ever had, even though we live in such different worlds. I liked having a taste of his world, I really liked it.

Now, I'm back in my own world, without him. The couch in our dorm's living area is the nicest spot in our apartment, but since I share it with seven other people, there's hardly a time when I could get it to myself.

This is one of those rare times. It's an afternoon when I have no classes, no private lessons and no job obligation. For the past few weeks, I would've spent an afternoon like this in either Kingston's penthouse or at the Abrams' mansion practicing on their grand piano, but I didn't feel like doing it today. When I called Wally to let her know that I'm not coming today, she sighed with disappointment. It was nice to hear that she likes me around because I've always worried about being a nuisance to her, but I still couldn't get myself to go there today.

The fact that Kingston didn't invite me to his place today is preying on my mind. Is he really done with me, just because I didn't agree to let him be my sugar daddy? I don't want to believe that. At the same time, I feel naive for thinking that it could've been anything else. I've heard the stories about him, I knew what he was like.

And I'm playing at his engagement party, for God's sake.

Still, I'm moping on the couch, staring at my phone's screen, hoping for a message from him.

When I hear the door opening, I lazily lift my head to see my roommate Kim walk in, carrying her violin. She usually has private lessons at this time, so I'm surprised to see her.

"No lesson today?" I ask.

Kim puts her violin down and sinks down on the couch next to me.

"Feeling too shitty," she says. "I think I might have caught something."

Now that she mentions it, she does look a little feverish.

"You want me to make you a tea?" I offer, but she shakes her head.

"I'm probably gonna' take a nap," she breathes. "As soon as I can get back up."

She pauses and turns her head to me. "What are you doing here? Not at the Abrams' residence today?"

"Feeling too shitty," I mimic her. It's an honest reply, but not the one she expected.

"What's wrong?" she wants to know. "You sick, too?"

She furls her eyebrows as she observes me, coming to a conclusion a few moments later.

"Nah, that's not it," she says. "You're just mopey. What's up?"

I can't tell her. Kim is the closest thing to a friend for me, but I can't even tell her. If she only makes the smallest comment to anyone here, it would feed Benjamin's nasty rumors. I can't risk that.

"It's complicated," I say, regretting it a moment later, as her eyes flicker with curiosity.

"Complicated?" she asks. "Like boy complicated?"

I sigh and throw her a look from the side. "You really have a nose for these things."

Kim shrugs. "What else could it be?"

She has a point there.

"Is it still Benjamin?" she wants to know. "Is he still giving you shit about leaving him?"

"I didn't *leave* him," I say. "We weren't even in a real relationship or anything."

Kim raises her hands in defense. "Okay, okay."

"It's not him," I add. "I actually talked to him. He seems to be doing better and as far as I know, he even stopped talking behind my back."

I look at her questioningly. "Or did you hear anything?"

Kim shakes her head.

"No, not really," she says. "But last I saw him, he didn't look very happy."

"Benjamin never looks happy," I say.

She chuckles. "That's true. He always has that frown on his face. Grumpy dude."

Kim shifts around on the cushions of the sofa and scans the living area, as if she's checking every door that leads to another bedroom, as if she wants to make sure we're alone.

"But it was different lately," she continues. "I saw him a few days ago and he looked as if he was ready to kill someone. That's why I thought you guys had another fight or something."

"Weird," I comment.

"So, you didn't even talk to him lately?" Kim asks.

I shake my head. "No. I haven't seen him in days. He's become very good at avoiding me."

"But you said you talked to him?"

"Yeah," I say. "But that's been a while ago. I tried to put things right between us."

"Hmmm," she says. "Maybe he found a new girl to be mad at."

"Let's hope!" I tell her. "I wouldn't mind one bit if he got his mind off of me."

Kim sighs and swipes across her forehead with the back of her hand.

"Hey, does that tea offer still stand?" she asks, looking at me with pleading eyes.

I smile at her.

"Of course," I say. "Peppermint or chamomile?"

CHAPTER XXVII

Kingston

This is the part I'm good at. Ghosting. I think that's what they call it. Ignore a girl's messages for long enough until she realizes that you're done with her. I've done it so many times before. There were very few times when I told a girl that I was done with her. Ghosting was usually my way to go. Is it the coward way out? Sure! But it's also the more convenient way, even more efficient in a way, because you don't have to deal with the emotional aftermath of a girl's broken heart.

Then why is it so hard this time? And on me?

When Elodie rejected my offer and thus denied the opportunity to get closer to her, I decided right there on the spot that this was it. It's the smartest thing to do. Gloria's warning may have made the forbidden fruit taste all the better, but that was just for the moment. I was deluded by that afternoon, that magical moment when she mesmerized me with her distinct beauty. She bewitched me.

I was ready to take more from Elodie than I've ever taken from any other girl, and when she put me in my place with that humiliating rejection, it was like a wake-up call.

You fucking idiot! What were you thinking? Get out of this now.

So, that's what I'm doing. But while I dreaded receiving any further messages from the other girls before, I now find myself checking my phone every few minutes, feeling relieved when there's a new message from Elodie and disappointed when there's not. I hate feeling this way. It's stupid. It's not me.

She does send me messages once in a while, but she's too proud and too strong to bombard me in the pathetic way that others have done before her. I expected nothing less of her.

I'm early for our weekly family dinner, and when I walk through the door, I can hear the familiar sound of Elodie playing upstairs. I knew that this is one of the days she practices here, but she's usually gone long before it's time for dinner. It's been a while since we've run into each other in this house. The last time that happened was when I first tasted her and surprised her with a kiss on the stairs as she was about to leave.

"Miss Hill is still here?" I ask, as Wally opens the door for me.

Wally looks at me with her usual maternal smile.

"You're early," she says. "And your mother and I agreed that her music is a nice background tune while we're finishing up preparations for dinner."

She closes the door behind me. "Does it disturb you?"

I shake my head. "No. I was just confused."

"Kingston," my mother greets me, approaching us in wide steps, a cloud of perfume accompanying her as she welcomes me with two kisses on the cheek.

"You're early," she says. "So unlike you."

"I can leave and come back, if you prefer," I tease her.

My mother is not one for sarcasm and just rolls her eyes at me.

"You didn't bring Gloria with you," she states.

"She'll join us later," I say.

Fuck knows where that girl is off to again. After telling me to be careful in regard to Elodie, she has been doing the exact opposite and acting even more stupid than before. I'm not sure I'm the one putting our arrangement in danger with the way she's behaving these days. With the way she blatantly flirts and hangs out with her group of friends at the clubs, it almost seems as if she wants everything to tank.

I just now realize that the music has stopped. If I don't get out of this entrance hall soon, I'll run right into Elodie when she comes down the stairs to leave the house - and I would very much like to avoid that.

But I'm not fast enough. Just as I hand my coat and scarf over to Wally, ready to move into the living room, I see my mother's and Wally's eyes move up the staircase.

Elodie is wearing another outfit that I gave her, a sleek mid-length knit dress that hugs her slim frame and adds just a hint of sexiness, a long side slit providing a sultry finish. She's wearing her hair up for a change and has painted her eyes in a smoky and darker style than usual. While she may look like pure innocence to everyone else, she radiates an irresistible allure to me.

Her green eyes widen when she sees me, and she walks down the stairs with careful and slow steps, uncertain what to do.

"Miss Hill," my mother pipes. "That sounded as beautiful as always. I can't wait to hear your performance at the engagement party."

Elodie casts a shy smile at her.

"Thank you, Mrs. Abrams," she says. "I'll be on my way."

Wally searches for Elodie's coat in the closet next to the entrance door, while we stand in an awkward triangle with my unsuspecting mother right next to me.

"Do you feel well-prepared?" my mother asks her. "For the event, I mean."

Elodie smiles at her. It's a distant and polite smile, overshadowed by a sadness for which I'm sure I'm to blame. While it makes her look incredibly beautiful, it causes my heart to ache in a way that's new to me.

"Yes," she says in a faint voice. "I think I've come up with a final playlist now. I can send it to you next week, if that's okay?"

My mother nods. "Sure, sure. That'll do. We have everything settled, so this should be good. And I reckon there will be no surprises on that list?"

Elodie shakes her head. "No, Ma'am."

She receives her coat from Wally and puts it on, avoiding eye contact with me at all times. With the way she's behaving right now, it's hard to believe that I've had her bent over in my apartment, begging for my cock more than once. I can still see her teary eyes, her shivering body every time I was done with her.

I want to do all of that to her again. Right now. And it makes me sick that I can't.

"If you don't mind," Elodie says, directed at my mother, "I think I won't need any further practice sessions here. If it's alright with you, I will see you on the day of the party?"

My mother raises her eyebrows in surprise.

"Yes, sure dear," she says. "But you know, you could still –"

"I'd rather not," Elodie says. "I'll be busy and I think I've burdened you enough."

My mother places her hand on Elodie's shoulder. "You've never been a burden, dear. On the contrary, we've enjoyed having you play here. Isn't that right?"

My mother is mostly speaking to Wally, but includes me in her search for confirmation, so I nod.

Elodie glances at me, her face stone cold and unreadable.

"I'll be on my way," she says in a faint voice.

"We will see you at the party," my mother says, while Wally opens the door for Elodie to leave.

"Goodbye, Miss Hill," I say, mostly to see whether she acknowledges me with any kind of attention.

Elodie looks up at me, her gaze darkening.

"Mrs. Abrams," she says, nodding toward me before she turns around and walks out the door.

Her voice and her look leave me with a throbbing pain in my chest. I have to fight every fiber of my being not to run after her, catching and wrapping her up in my arms and claiming her with a kiss that could lead to so much more.

And what the hell is that dumb lump in my throat?

"I'm going to miss her," Wally says after she closes the door behind Elodie. "I've grown so accustomed to her wonderful music."

My mother clears her throat. "Yes, it was nice to have some artistic touch in this home."

I follow them into the kitchen, sitting at the countertop while I watch Wally finishing up on dinner preparations and my mother filling her glass with wine. It's a typical scene from my upbringing. These two women, talking in the kitchen while one of them works, the other drinks, while I sit at the counter, watching them. Today is one of the rare occasions where my mother decides to share her wine with me. She places a glass in front of me, casting me a quick look as she does.

"How are you doing?" she asks, taking a seat next to me. "Nervous about tying the knot?"

I look at her, wondering if she truly believes that Gloria is the woman of my dreams, the woman I love. The woman I'm looking forward to spending the rest of my life with.

"Not really," I tell her, sipping on my wine. "Everything seems to be going according to plan. The flowers, the food, the location. The music."

My mother takes a sip of her own drink, nodding quietly. Wally is standing with her back to us, blending the dressing for our appetizers and appearing overly focused on it. She's been working for our family for a very long time. Even if it had ever been my mother's intention, she probably couldn't have managed to hide even our dirtiest secrets from her. Wally knows everything, but she never talks about anything.

"Yes, things are all set for the party," my mother says, sounding bored. "But you know that's not what I'm talking about."

She casts me a look from the side, her right eyebrow raised.

"I guess I'm as nervous as anybody who's about to get married," I say.

"Look, Kingston," my mother says, swirling the liquid in her glass. "I know you don't love Gloria, and I know she doesn't love you."

I huff. "No secret about that, huh?"

She throws me a warning look.

"Believe it or not, son, I would've wanted things to be different for you," she says. "But with the way you've been behaving, it's become hard for your father to trust you with his legacy."

I huff again. "His legacy? If anything, it's my grandfather's legacy, and he's about to fuck up everything. You and I both know that."

Actually, I'm not sure if my mother does know this, but I'm curious to hear her opinion about it. She's not really involved in my father's business, but she's neither stupid nor blind. She's been at those dinner meetings, she's sat with the men while they were discussing my father's many mistakes and shortcomings, and she must know about the financial trouble we're facing if our family's shipping empire doesn't adjust to modern times and updates its systems in the near future. We've already lost too many clients, too many contracts that had been in place for a long time before my father took over.

"Darling, if I didn't know about it, I wouldn't force you to go through with a wedding that lacks the love and passion one would otherwise want," she says without looking at me. "I know you're giving up a lot for this, and I know there might be more suitable options out there. More suitable for the heart, that is."

Even Wally pauses at my mother's somber tone. She never speaks like this, and I'm just as surprised as Wally to witness her unusual demeanor.

"I'm very proud of you for doing this," she says, now looking at me. "I know it may be a silly demand coming from your father and me, but it's time for you to act like a man. God knows we can't rely on your brother to do it."

"Acting like a man," I repeat, my voice underlined with a bitter tone. "My ability to run this company shouldn't have to rely on me entering a loveless marriage with a Waldorf girl I barely know."

"You know Gloria well enough," my mother says. "The Waldorf's are a family of great influence, you couldn't ask for a better match."

She pauses and our eyes meet.

"If this was a business deal, I'd agree," I tell her.

My mother shrugs. "You know marriages served to save kingdoms in earlier times. You're doing nothing less with this."

The doorbell rings and Wally hurries to the door as if she can't wait to escape our conversation. My mother gets up from her seat as well, casting me a look as if to tell me that our little chat better stay between us.

I watch as she walks away and wonder if saving a kingdom is really worth this ugly charade.

CHAPTER XVIII

Elodie

S o, this was it then? Kingston really seems to be done with me, whether I like it or not. I've stopped sending him messages after the last time we ran into each other at his parents' house. I wonder if he showed up early that night to see me.

But if he did, he made no effort to talk to me in private. On the contrary, he treated me with such cold distance that it's hard to believe the things that happened between us ever happened.

It's better this way. No matter how great things felt between us, we both knew this couldn't go on forever. The longer it would have lasted, the harder it would have been to stop.

Soon, this will all be forgotten. I just have to get through this one night, the engagement party. Mrs. Abrams has already asked me whether I'd be willing to perform at the actual wedding as well, but I've told her that I'll need more time to consider. Of course, I really need that gig. I need the money and the visibility.

It's always been my dream to make it as a solo pianist, and I would love to build a career as a freelance artist who gets hired for events of this kind, but I know how hard it is to make this work. And I don't have wealthy parents who could support me while trying to fulfill my dream, like a lot of my fellow students at Juilliard do. I have to make money right away and get my foot in the door as early as possible.

I knew this could be the chance to do just that, and if it means I have to perform while watching the man I was falling in love with tying the knot with another woman, then so be it.

"Falling in love with?" I give voice to my thoughts, whispering to myself while getting ready in my room.

I'm standing in front of our mirror, staring at myself as if I was faced with my own reflection for the very first time.

As if this was a stranger looking back at me.

Kingston gave me a taste of something I never thought was possible for myself. He gave me taste of true passion, true desire, the ability to explore another side of myself. He let me have a taste of his lavish world and the bliss of being at the receiving end of his skills as a lover.

Now all of that is gone. And tonight I have to play for him and his fiancée and congratulate them on a union that I know is nothing but a business deal, one that steals him away from me.

I hate this, but I have to go through with it.

The dress he bought for me is still the most expensive and most lavish outfit I own, so that's what I decided to wear tonight. As I stand in front of the mirror, checking myself for the last time before I leave the house, I find myself faced with a challenge I didn't see coming when I took this job a few months ago.

I have to deliver the performance of my life, while my heart feels as if it's shattering into pieces.

This sucks.

It doesn't get better when I leave my room and walk into the last person I need to see right now. Benjamin is sitting on our sofa in the living room, jumping up as he sees me walking out.

"Leaving for your big gig?" he asks.

I stop mid-pace and turn to him, furling my eyebrows. Knowing him, I don't expect any well wishes for tonight.

"Yes," I say, ready to leave it at that, but he won't let me.

"That can't be easy," he says, approaching me. "Watching your favorite sugar daddy get hitched to a woman who plays in a different league than you."

I swallow hard and try to appear more appalled than shocked at his accusation.

"You've got to stop making up this shit about me, Benjamin," I hiss at him. "Now excuse me, I –"

"I know I'm not making this one up!" he barks at me, blocking my way to the door. "I saw you! You and him!"

My heart almost stops, and I know he can see it in my face. Now it's impossible for me to hide my shock at what he's saying.

"That's right," he says, narrowing his eyes as he casts an evil smirk at me. "I saw you with him. I know you're fucking him, and I know he's the one who paid for this dress and all the other fancy clothes you've been showboating lately."

How? How the hell does he know this? How the hell did he see us?

Of course, I can't ask him that because it would give away that he's right. But I don't know what else to say, so we just remain in a stare contest for a few more moments before I try to break free again.

"You're out of your mind," I say, trying to get past him.

Benjamin blocks my way with his arm.

"I'm not," he objects. "We both know what I say is true. And we both know that this does not bode well for you. If I tell anyone, the Abrams family, Mrs. Bellamy... you're fucking screwed, Elodie."

I bite my lower lip, trembling with fury and fear while I fight back the tears. I can't cry now, it would ruin my makeup and I would look like a scarecrow when I show up for my job at the party.

"I can just imagine their faces when I tell them," he continues. "How you dragged your little sugar daddy into that coffee place, so he can fuck you where you'd normally serve tables. Did you guys get off on that? The fact that he was doing you at your shitty work place?"

His words make me feel sick to my stomach. He's spewing so much hate. I can't believe we'd been more than close friends just a few months ago.

"How sad are you," I whisper, avoiding eye contact with him. "Are you stalking me? How can you be so obsessed to be following me around like this?"

Benjamin huffs. "Still not admitting it, are you?"

"What do you want?" I ask, looking up at him through narrow eyes. "What the hell do you want from me, Benjamin? Do you really hate me this much?"

He glares at me.

"I want you to own up to it," he says. "Own up to the fact that you're a fucking slut."

His words hurt. I wish I could be stronger and just brush his insult away as if it was nothing to me.

But I can't.

The worst thing about his accusation is that I don't even disagree completely. I've hooked up with a man who's about to get married, a man who's filthy rich and who showered me with presents, even though I never asked for it. I feel bad for what I've done, and having Benjamin pointing it out like this only adds to my distraught.

"I don't have time for this," I say. "You need to grow the fuck up, Benjamin."

He looks at me with that same face of disgust as before, but moves aside to let me through.

"You better be careful, Elodie," he says as I'm about to leave. "That's a pretty deep hole you've dug for yourself."

CHAPTER XXIX

Kingston

This is harder than I thought it would be. I'm standing next to Gloria, greeting guests as they enter the venue, hiding behind a facade, a person that I don't feel connected to at all.

Gloria is hanging onto my arm, styled to the nines with her hair put up, overloaded with ostentatious jewelry and makeup that's so heavy it's hard to tell what her face looks like behind it. While she's as much of a liar as I am, I expected her to use this evening and the wedding itself as a stage for her narcissist nature. All eyes will be on her, everybody who walks in congratulates her first before they turn to me. This evening is all about the bride-to-be, and while she's not in love with the man who makes her a bride, it's still a chance for her to be princess for a day.

Yet, she's not acting that way.

I expected her to gloat and beam all evening, boasting that fake smile while she bathes in the attention. Instead, she's hanging onto my arm, forcing a smile every time she has to shake a hand, but displaying a rather gloomy expression as soon as no one is looking directly at her. She barely talked to me, which is not unusual in itself, but it's weird that she doesn't even give me snarky comments like she usually does. If I didn't know any better, I'd think that she's regretting this decision.

Well, it's a little bit too late for that, girl.

Tonight is the night where our arrangement is pretty much sealed in front of all the eyes of the Upper East Side that matter. I'm ignoring the lump in my throat as that thought settles in my chest with a nauseating discomfort.

Tonight's guests are what our families call 'close friends', but I don't really know most of them, let alone feel close to anyone.

Except one person.

She's sitting at the grand piano in a corner at the far back of the ballroom, playing ambient music while the guests are arriving. Elodie and I haven't spoken one word or even exchanged a look tonight, but I can feel her presence every moment. I feel drawn to her and it's almost physically painful that I can't just walk up to her, touch her, kiss her, bend her over that piano lid and fuck her like I did in my home a few weeks ago.

I miss her. God, I miss her.

She's wearing the dress I bought for her and has curled her brown locks in a way that I've never seen before. Her lips are painted red and her green eyes framed with thick black mascara. I prefer less paint on her porcelain face, but she looks more beautiful than any other woman in the room nonetheless. The way she's so deeply immersed in the music she's playing is the most alluring sight.

"Geoffrey," I hear Gloria piping next to me. "It's good to see you."

The way her voice jumps up as she says his name catches my attention, and I pull my eyes away from Elodie.

Geoffrey Goldbaum, the son of one of my father's associates, is standing in front of us with his parents. He looks like a fucking Disney prince with his blond locks and that obnoxious smile that exposes his too white teeth. I've never liked the guy. There's just something about him. That sleazy attitude, that fake smile, those damn teeth - and the fact that he's everybody's darling even though his nocturnal adventures have been very similar to mine for years. Somehow he manages to keep up the good guy image, while it's apparent to anyone that *I'm* the bad boy who needs to be tamed with a fixed-up wife. However, he cares more about his image than I ever did.

He casts a grin at Gloria that would make any other husband-to-be next to her explode with jealousy, and that look is reciprocal. Gloria lets out a silly giggle as he takes her hand, planting a kiss on the back of it. The way they look at each other is sickening.

"You're fucking him, aren't you," I whisper to her once Mr. Goldilocks and his parents are out of earshot.

Gloria inhales audibly and looks at me, her eyes wide with indignation. "Excuse me?"

"Oh, come on," I say, rolling my eyes. "It's so obvious."

She huffs. "What do you care?"

I raise my eyebrows at her. "Weren't you the one to remind me that we're about to get married?"

Gloria huffs again, shaking her head and scanning our surroundings to make sure that no one is overhearing our whispered conversation.

"So, it's okay for you to fuck that timid nerd over there, but I can't have fun of my own?" she asks, nodding toward Elodie at the other end of the room.

"Not if you think you can threaten me without repercussions," I hiss at her. "His father works with mine and so does he, which means that I will work closely with him in the very near future. You're threatening this deal way more than I ever have!"

Gloria pouts, something that would look cute on almost any other woman's face, but just makes her look like the affronted brat she is.

We're interrupted by my mother, who emerges next to me, placing her hand on my shoulder to catch my attention.

"Kingston, Gloria," she says in that polite but distant tone she reserves for public occasions such as this one. "I believe most of the guests are here now. I think it's okay for you two to take your seats."

She adds a little warning look as she sends us off, causing me to worry that she might have overheard our conversation before, or even parts of it.

Gloria and I follow her gesture and walk over to our seats at the head of the main table.

I glance over to Elodie as we approach our seats, but she's too immersed in her music and doesn't look my way once, not even for a second. Even though her music radiates through the entire ballroom, I'm the only person who pays attention to her. Before meeting her, I'd never wasted a thought on the musicians who accompany events like this, so I'm not surprised that she goes completely overlooked by the guests tonight.

But I can't help staring at her. Every time my obligations force me to withdraw my attention from her, it's accompanied by a painful sting.

And as I look at Gloria, I can't help but think that she might be feeling the same way about the blond pompadour. As much as I despise her, the somber mood of her is palpable tonight, and I've never seen her like that.

It's almost as if she's miserably in love.

CHAPTER XXX

Elodie

I t was easy while I was playing the piano. I have a very strict schedule, taped to the back of one of my sheets that includes almost every minute of tonight's event. It's a detailed timetable for the entire three hours that this engagement party is supposed to last, showing me when the evening asks for music and when it's time for me to pause. The pauses are mainly reserved for speeches, and I'm filled with horror when I see Kingston listed as one of the speakers.

Of course he is. He's the groom.

Mrs. Abrams asked me to accompany the first few minutes of the evening while the guests are arriving, but since this is the only part that's not written out in detail on the schedule she gave me, I don't know exactly when to stop. As a result, I just keep playing tune after tune, some of which I don't really like. I've had to choose a few songs that I'm sick of personally, but that I know are still very suitable for an evening like this and popular with people who haven't heard them over and over again like I have. I decided to play most of them in the early minutes of the evening, so that I have something to look forward to as the night progresses.

I've dreaded this evening, but even the worst thoughts that have occurred to me in regard to tonight don't come close to how horrible it turns out to be right now. I can see Kingston and Gloria standing at the door, greeting their guests while she has her arm tucked into his. There's no satisfaction for me in seeing that neither of them look happy. I've only met Gloria twice, but she's never seemed as reserved as she does tonight.

Is she regretting this?

It may make me a terrible person, but a part of me wants to see her break tonight. In the darkest corners of my mind, I'm envisioning a dramatic outburst on her part, a scene in which she cries and yells, putting an end to this sick arrangement and freeing Kingston of his obligation.

And then I remember that he wouldn't even want that. He's in this for a reason, and if she breaks the deal, it will only put him in more trouble, but it won't mean that he'll declare his love for me and take me home on a white stallion, riding into the sunset as a happy couple.

He's done with me no matter what.

Mrs. Abrams comes up to the piano, gesturing for me to stop after the current song. I nod at her and skip the last repetition to bring the song to an earlier end. If I remember correctly, the evening will start with a welcoming speech by Gloria's father.

I have zero interest in listening to that, but I also have no idea where to go. Mrs. Abrams told me that there would be breaks for me during the speeches, but she never mentioned if there was any place for me to go.

So, I just stay where I feel the safest, on my piano bench, partly hidden behind the instrument that is my life, with my hands resting in my lap instead of traveling along the keys.

I notice that Kingston and Gloria are no longer standing at the door, but have taken their seats at the main table. They're sitting in the middle, surrounded by their parents to the left and right. The table is placed along the wall opposite the piano, allowing them to face me and the rest of the room.

And Kingston is looking directly at me.

Our eyes meet for the first time this evening, and his dark gazes feels as if he's choking me. He's not smiling, but just displaying a stone cold expression that doesn't let me read anything into it. In a way, I'm glad that he's not smiling at me because it would feel as if he's mocking me. As if this is all just a big joke to him.

Clearly, it's not.

It's a relief to see that he's suffering, too. But it makes me angry at the same time. Why the hell is he doing this? There must be another way? How can he let his parents dictate such a major part of his life?

I want to avert my eyes from him, but I can't. Our eyes remain locked onto each other across the room, even when his father gets up from his seat and calls for everybody's attention by clanging a spoon against his glass. I don't listen to his speech, but continue to stare at Kingston as if I was waiting for an explanation. And he stares back.

His father's speech is tedious and long, and I sigh with relief when Mrs. Abrams signals for me to continue playing. The evening drags on, but it's so much easier as long as I can keep my eyes on the keys in front of me, focusing on the music, doing what I love. Music has always been my best solace, my companion when there was no one else. It's also a reminder of the loneliness I've had to endure all my life. My father never understood this passion, all he saw in it was a threat, a threat that would take away the money he reserved for drinking, a threat to his daughter's future, because becoming an artist is not a lucrative career choice.

I press my lips together as I think of him and his constant accusations. I wish he could see me now. He would hate every part of it, those filthy rich snobs, their ridiculous get-ups, the speeches, the tiny food portions, the decoration, the silly music. He would hate it because it shows him quite plainly how pitiful he is. Yes, artists may struggle, and yes, it's not the most lucrative career choice, but it certainly beats being a deadbeat alcoholic.

I've fought hard for this, and my efforts are finally starting to pay off. If a broken heart is what I'll have to endure to reach my goal, then so be it. I can do this. I know I can.

The schedule calls for another pause when the first course is announced, but I'm asked to continue playing while everyone eats. With every minute that passes, we're getting closer to the moment when Kingston will have to give his speech. He will speak after the main course and hand over to Gloria right after so she can announce the dessert. What a silly display this all is.

I'm now moving on to some of my favorite pieces, some of Chopin's Nocturnes, Schubert's Serenade, the Adagio from one of Scriabin's Sonatas. They're all calm, but very melancholic in nature. I chose them for this time of the evening because I knew they'd reflect my mood as I anticipate Kingston's speech. It's my little secret that the sadness portrayed in these pieces is my own.

I don't even notice the single tear running down my cheek until I'm asked to stop playing. My hands are resting on the final chord of the heavy piece, still fading away when I look up to see Kingston standing up, looking at me as if he just saw a ghost. He's holding up his glass, staring at me with his mouth partly opened and his eyes unusually wide. Another tear travels down my face and I hurry to wipe it away.

I'm still hoping for a miracle. That dramatic outburst, a moment of weakness during which either Gloria or Kingston loses it and calls the whole thing off, showing the guests how idiotic this whole spectacle really is.

But it's not happening. Kingston grabs a hold of himself, clearing his throat and tearing his eyes away from me to face the rest of the room, an audience of at least a hundred people, most of them now looking up at him in expectation.

I remain on my seat, my hands resting in my lap and my shoulders tense as I fight back the tears. No one is paying attention to me, and even if they were, my tears could be interpreted as tears of emotion for the happy couple. But I don't want to give him this satisfaction. I don't want him to see how much this is hurting me. Not if he keeps playing along like this.

And he does. When he begins speaking, it becomes crystal clear to me that there will be no miracle tonight. There will be no surprise outburst, no rebellion, no chance for us. Kingston speaks in a formal tone, thanking the guests for coming, addressing the food, the location, and the music. He nods toward me as he mentions the piano accompaniment, causing a few heads to turn my way. I don't feel comfortable with this kind of attention and glare back at him for being such a heartless puppet. When his eyes meet mine, I see nothing in them. It's like he's a different person.

"... to celebrate this union," he concludes another sentence, placing his hand on Gloria's shoulder. She smiles absentmind-edly and lifts her hand, placing it on his to give the impression that there's some kind of emotional bond between them.

I choke.

No, not now. I feel like a cold clamp as been placed around my heart, closing around it and painfully squeezing every bit of emotion out of it. I feel sick to my stomach, and my vision blurs as a new wave of tears threatens to dampen my face.

I'm either going to throw up or wail any moment now. I don't know which will be first, but I know I can do neither here.

Kingston is still speaking when I jump up from my bench, causing heads to turn to me again. His eyes are not the only ones following me as I dart out of the ballroom, making my awkwardly long way to the French doors at the entrance area while hiding most of my face with my right hand pressed against my mouth.

CHAPTER XXXI

Kingston

I tried. I really tried. I tried to act like the man my parents expect me to be today. I did everything within my power.

But this is too much. It was hard enough to watch Elodie look at me, tears running down her face after she finished what I know to be one of her favorite Nocturnes. Her music was hard to listen to because it was a clear telltale of her pain. I'm sure I'm the only one who didn't mistake her melancholic tunes for just that, a calm and gentle background music. It's not only the music itself, but the she way she played it, the way she carried herself while her hands were traveling along the keyboard. I've seen her play before, I know what she looks like when she's in a good place.

This was not it. There was no swaying along with the music, no expression on her face. She just followed the notes, almost robotic and slower than some of the parts were intended to be played.

I tried to look away, and I succeeded in that, most of the time. But I couldn't play deaf.

And I can't ignore her now. She's not causing a scene, I know she's running out of the room because she wants to avoid just that. She doesn't want people to see her distraught because she can no longer hide it behind her performance.

I'm just about to wrap up the hardest part of tonight, my dreaded dinner speech, when she jumps up from her bench, trying to hide her tortured face while she runs out. She's doing it quietly and so quickly that she's already out the door by the time most people realize that anything out of the ordinary is going on.

"Is she sick?" I hear my mother whisper from the side.

My eyes are glued to the door through which Elodie just escaped. It would be easy to gloss over this if I just continued to speak. I could wrap up this speech, raise my glass, thank everyone and hand over the microphone to Gloria so she can do the same.

It would be so easy.

But I can't. The hand in which I'm holding the microphone sinks down on its own, and I turn to Gloria next to me. She's looking up at me, raising her eyebrows and speaking a silent threat with her widened eyes. Everything in her gaze warns me to do this. She'll get Elodie fired, she'll ruin her reputation, she'll ruin Elodie's career - and me.

I agreed to this so I could finally take over my father's job as the head of our shipping empire and save it from ruin. I know it's a worthy goal, and it's necessary to save my family's fortune. Nothing has changed in that regard.

Except for me. I have changed.

I will save my family's company, and I will "act like a man".

But I will have to find another way to do it.

I drop the microphone on the table.

"Kingston," Gloria hisses as she realizes what I'm about to do.

However, she doesn't try to hold me back when I turn and walk away in wide and determined strides. No one tries to call me back. These people are all too afraid of causing a scene. They'll sit quietly and act as if nothing happened, while Gloria will most likely find a way to distract them with her own speech. Or my father. My mother. Her parents.

I don't care about any of this.

All I care about is finding Elodie and putting an end to her agony.

I sigh in relief when I walk through the French doors, turning right as she did when she left. This is when I start running, following the long hallway, passing the cloakroom and cursing at myself for waiting this long. The hallway leads to a big and open staircase and I have no idea where to go from here. She could be anywhere.

I come to a halt at the staircase, looking around, wondering what to do next, when I hear a sound to my left. Stone pillars are placed around the hall for decorations and behind one of them, I can see a fair-skinned elbow peeking out.

"Elodie?" I ask, approaching the pillar.

A faint sob is all I hear and when I walk around the pillar, I find her hiding away from me, hunched over and both her hands pressed against her face while she weeps uncontrollably.

"Go away," she tells me, muffled by her hands. "Go, go, go."

She flinches away when I touch her shoulders and try to pull her closer.

"Elodie, please look at me," I say.

She shakes her head and tries to evade my touch.

"Go back," she pleads. "Go away."

"Please, Elodie, listen –"

"No!" she yells, removing her hands and looking up at me through teary eyes. "You don't need to explain. I'm okay. Please, I don't need to hear anything. I know, I know."

She sniffs and takes a deep breath.

"I'll finish my job," she adds. "Just give me a minute. I'll be okay."

I shake my head.

"No, you don't know," I object. "I'm not going to do this."

She looks at me, her eyes widening with disbelief. "What?"

"I can't go through with it," I say. "I thought I could. I thought I had to. But I can't."

She furls her eyebrows, wiping away another tear before she sniffs again, trying to regain composure. It hurts to see her like this, I just want to make it stop. I've never felt like this when I was confronted with a crying woman. Usually, they'd just annoy the hell out of me and I'd try everything to get away from them.

Elodie just proves once again that she's different. She didn't use her tears to get her way, but instead tried to hide them from me and everybody else, suffering in hiding, too proud and too scared to let anyone see how much this is hurting her.

How much I'm hurting her.

"But…but your family," she whispers. "You… can't."

"I'm a grown man, Elodie," I say. "I'll find a way. It'll work out, it has to, because I can't marry Gloria. It's not worth this."

"Bu –"

She's interrupted by the sound of fast clicking high heels coming from down the hallway and stops speaking as I look around the pillar to see Gloria approaching us in wide and angry steps.

"What the hell, Kingston!" she yells, pointing at me. "You and your little slut –"

"Hey!" I interrupt her, my voice so pervasive that both she and Elodie wince in shock. "Watch your tongue for once, Gloria!"

Gloria comes to a halt right next to us and I instinctively move myself in front of Elodie to protect her from that witch's fury. But Elodie wouldn't be herself if she let that happen. She touches my arm as she steps forward to stand her ground.

Gloria glares at her just for a second before she turns back to me.

"What the hell were you thinking," she hisses at me. "How could you not let me in on this!"

Both, Elodie and I gasp in surprise, exchanging a quick look before I address Gloria.

"What?" I ask, frowning at her. "Let you in on what?"

"This!" she says, pointing back and forth between Elodie and me. "If you're that serious with your little ch –"

I raise my eyebrow as a warning and Gloria pauses, clearing her throat before she continues to speak.

"Why didn't you tell me that you'd be staging this little play?" she asks. "And that you were planning to call the wedding off?"

"We didn't stage anything," I tell her. "And I didn't plan to call anything off."

I pause and look at Elodie. "Until now."

Gloria huffs. "You should've told me, Kingston. After all we've been through together, this is just not fair."

"Told you what?" I bark at her.

"That you're serious with her," Gloria says, waving at Elodie.

"The last time we talked you threatened to fire Elodie if I don't stop this!" I remind her.

"What?" Elodie interjects, looking back and forth between Gloria and me.

"Oh, whatever," Gloria says, rolling her eyes. "I just didn't want you have to have… this."

Gloria pauses with an unusual expression of insecurity on her face.

"I didn't like the idea of you having something that I can't have," she finally admits. "When I threatened you… that was before –"

"You got serious with Geoffrey Goldilocks?" I ask her. "Or before he got serious with you?"

Even under all the heavy layers of makeup, I can tell that Gloria is blushing. She opens her mouth in an attempt to say something, but no words come out. Instead, she just adds more huffing noises, her eyes scanning the hall as if she could find an answer there.

"It's true, isn't it?" I ask her. "I'm not the only one who fell in love with someone else."

"What?" Elodie breathes next to me.

Fuck. Did I really just say that?

Gloria raises one of her eyebrows, casting me a mischievous smirk.

I try to ignore her and turn to Elodie, who's staring up at me, her eye makeup is smeared from crying and her hair is a mess, strands of it sticking to the dried-up tears on her cheeks. Her lower lip is trembling, and so are her talented hands.

"You... love me?" she asks with a voice so low that it's barely audible.

I don't know. I don't fucking know what it feels like to love someone. Why the hell did I just say that?

Why does my tongue feel so dry? Is the building spinning? I feel dizzy. Did they put something in our drinks?

"I-I, well, I mean it's —"

"Oh, for fuck's sake, Kingston," Gloria hisses next to me. "Be a man for once."

"Shut up!" I bark at her. "This is not... why are you even here?"

Now, both of them are looking at me as if I've lost my mind.

Gloria rolls her eyes at me again.

"We don't have time for this. We have to tell these people something," she says, gesturing behind herself to the hallway. "They're waiting for an explanation, and I'm not going back in there by myself."

She has a point. We will have to explain this together. But explain what?

"What do you want to tell them?" I ask her.

Gloria purses her lips and cocks her head to the side.

"That the wedding is off," she says as if it's the most apparent thing to say. "What else?"

"So, I was right," I assume. "You want the wedding off?"

She shrugs. "You don't?"

I nod hesitantly. This seems almost too easy, even though I know it won't be, even if Gloria is as willing to go along as she appears to be right now.

"What will you tell your parents?" I ask her. "This deal was for your sake, too."

"You see, Kingston," Gloria says, going to back to the snarky tone that I'm used to. "It's a lot easier for me because I can replace you. Geoffrey is just as good a match as you are, and he'd be willing to take your place. We've already talked about it."

I furl my eyebrows at her. "You can't be serious."

"Surprised?" she asks, arching her eyebrows provocatively. "To be honest, if you guys hadn't performed this little scene in front of everybody, we probably would have."

She pauses and throws an annoyed look at Elodie.

"It just bugs me that you went first," she says. "Have you never thought about how this will make me look?"

Elodie frowns at her, but doesn't say a word.

"Now I look like the poor, lost woman who got cheated on right before her wedding, and –"

I can't help but laugh at her words, causing Gloria to stop mid-sentence. She throws me a dark look.

"Anyone who knows you will know that that's far from the truth," I say. "Don't worry, I'll handle this."

CHAPTER XXXII

Elodie

Kingston told me that it would be okay for me not to head back into the engagement party, but I objected. I needed to face the mess that I had created. Also, there was a part of me that still couldn't believe what had just happened. I'd been hoping for a crazy outburst, tears, people yelling and calling off the wedding in a dramatic scene. And then it happened... just not in the way I expected.

There will always be that nagging question inside of me, what would have happened if I hadn't run out of the ballroom during Kingston's speech. Would Gloria really have done what she said she'd do? She was to speak right after Kingston. Was that the moment she was waiting for to tell people that she no longer wanted to marry him?

She blamed me for making her look bad, but I can't feel too bad about it. Especially not after the scene she displayed once we walked back into the ballroom, all eyes instantly turning in our direction, followed by exasperated gasps and exclamations when Kingston opened his arms as if he was welcoming the entire room and announcing that he and Gloria had just decided to cancel their wedding plans. I believe Gloria's mother even fainted.

The awkward tension that spread through the room was only worsened by the yelling fathers, who jumped up from their seats and started accusing each other of having the worst and most unreliable offspring ever.

No one ever looked at me, no one asked about the connection between me leaving the room, and Gloria and Kingston deciding to call off their wedding.

No one but Mrs. Abrams.

I caught her eyes from far across the room, looking at me and... smiling. She was *smiling*. I was too puzzled to react in any way and just averted my eyes, putting a little distance between me and Kingston, just to make sure that there were no assumptions when we weren't ready to be open about whatever we had become now.

This was almost a week ago. Kingston and I haven't seen each other since that day, but we have talked a lot. We've texted and talked on the phone about everything - except one thing. I couldn't bring myself to confront him about that one thing he said while he was yelling at Gloria.

That thing about being in love with someone else, with me. I'm too afraid to ask him about that one.

Also, I was as busy as always because I couldn't afford to put my life on hold just because of that unexpected development at the engagement party.

Meanwhile, Kingston tried his best to deal with the fury of his father. I'm glad I wasn't involved in those fights, but from what he told me, it must have been awful. His father won't back off from his position, and if anything, it has only gotten worse now that Kingston and Gloria made "such fools of themselves and their families", as he called it. I feel terrible for causing him all this trouble, even though I know that marrying Gloria wouldn't have made him happy. But at least it would've enabled him to gain the respect he needs from his father to be able to become his successor.

I'm not a good match. I know I can't replace a Gloria Waldorf in that regard. I have no money, no big family name, no connections, no esteem.

It's no surprise that Kingston hasn't mentioned me in front of his parents. He told me that he no longer wants us to be a secret, but there's a time and place to tell his parents, and that time hasn't come yet.

He asked to see me on my next free afternoon, which is today. It feels like we're going on our first real date, and in a way, we are. I'm nervous and took forever to doll myself up, watched and mocked by Kim, who now knows about me and Kingston. I reckoned that it would only be a matter of time before Benjamin started spreading nasty rumors about me being the reason for the cancelation of the Abrams-Waldorf wedding, so I figured I should be one step ahead of him, even though he doesn't seem to have told anyone at this point.

I've been at Kingston's beautiful penthouse home so many times before, but today everything seems new and special. It's already dark by the time we walk inside and the place is bathed in dim and warm lights, with a candlelight dinner waiting for us on the dining table close to the open kitchen.

"You cooked?" I ask, half jokingly.

"You sound surprised," he says, while helping me out of my coat. "What makes you think I can't cook?"

"I didn't say that. It just... surprises me."

He chuckles and puts my coat away, gesturing for me to take a seat.

"Well, you can calm down," he says, placing a kiss on my neck before he moves the chair for me to sit down. "I just ordered us some sushi."

I sit down, watching as he walks around the table, preparing two glasses of champagne and giving me one of them before he sits down himself, opposite me.

He's looking dashingly handsome tonight, all dressed up in a black suit with a silver tie, his hair gelled to the side and his dark eyes reflecting an ease that I haven't seen on him before.

"I just realized I've never properly fed you when you were here," he says, raising his glass to me. "It's time for that to change."

We clink glasses and I can't help but feel so utterly awkward about all of this. He makes my heart flutter, and it only seems to have gotten worse since the first time we hooked up.

"Well, thank you," I say, helping myself to the first of many sushi rolls that are laid out on the table for us. "This is delicious!"

He smiles at me, and it's the cutest expression I could imagine. He has never looked at me like this, like a young boy on his first date, shy but yet confident. I know he's hungry for me, and the need is reciprocal. It's been too long since I've felt his strong and skillful hands on me.

"Are you doing okay?" he asks. "I hope your week has been better than mine."

I hesitate, my gaze darkening for a moment as I'm reminded of all the trouble he had to go through, while I haven't really faced any repercussions so far.

"You know my life has been less affected by this," I say. "I've had classes, working at the coffee place, practice. All the usual, except for the lack of practicing hours at the Abrams residence."

He chuckles. "Yeah, Wally and my mother both miss you."

"Your mother?" I ask. "But she doesn't know that-?"

"I think she has known for a while," he says, interrupting me. "She hasn't said anything to that effect, but she doesn't have to. The fact alone that she's defending me in front of my father is telltale enough."

He pauses to indulge on another maki roll before he continues.

"But she's mentioned you," he adds. "A lot. Saying how much she misses your music, and how she's concerned about you, now that you've lost a potential appointment now that there's no wedding."

I let out an awkward laugh. "She's worried about me?"

He nods. "I wouldn't say worried, but interested. As am I."

He puts his chopsticks aside and leans back in his chair, taking another sip from his champagne.

"Tell me," he says. "What is it you want to do after you're done with Juilliard? You're graduating soon, aren't you?"

I'm a bit taken aback at his interest in my career, and I can feel how my mind is turning to defense mode right away. Every time I've been asked that question before, it was by someone who objected to my interest in a musical career, with my father leading the way. There is a reason why I have barely spoken to him in recent years, as he made it very clear that he'd be done with me if I chose to follow a fruitless path and will no longer be his obligation.

Of course, my teachers and mentors at Juilliard were different. But while their advice was more supportive, they also had to act as the voice of reason, stopping me every time I dared to dream of a freelance career as a solo pianist. It can't be done, at least not for people like me who have no financial support or a valuable network of wealthy clients.

"Well, it's really not that easy," I tell him. "It's hard to make it as an artist. I could play in an orchestra, or become a teacher myself, or-"

"I'm asking what it is you *want*," he insists. "Not what you *could* do. What do you want to do, Elodie?"

I look at him, unsure whether I dare to be honest. No one has ever asked me that, not like this.

"I want to be a solo pianist," I say blatantly. "I want to be a freelancer, focusing on classical arrangements for high-end events and performances at private and public events."

Kingston nods. "So, events like the wedding that never happened?"

I smirk at him. "I'd prefer to play for happy couples, but yes, events like that. Or fundraisers, birthdays, anniversaries. You know, the kind that keeps families like yours busy."

Kingston eats another sushi roll and nods.

"Yeah, I'm familiar with the kind," he says. "I just never liked them. I can't imagine why anyone would want to be a part of them if they don't have to."

I smile and take another sip of the heavenly champagne he opened up for us. I will never get used to delicacies like this, and I'm glad about that. My poor upbringing and the struggles of my years at Juilliard may have been tough, but all of it made me the person I am today. A person who truly enjoys the luxuries a life with a man like Kingston offers.

"You and I grew up very differently," I remind him. "But I see where you're coming from. I don't know if I would enjoy them as much as a guest. But it's different when I get to play my music. As a musician, I help to create that atmosphere people want for their celebrations. Like a painter who can draw a world that only exists in his head, or a writer who brings a story to life with his words - a musician provides that final touch that makes an occasion special."

I pause, trying to find the right words to conclude my stream of thought.

"Artists are always expressive in nature, even when they like to hide behind their instrument, like a pianist does," I say. "While I do mostly play for myself, I need the satisfaction of having people listen to me. I want to share the music I love. Being able to do that... I consider that a privilege."

Kingston raises his eyebrows as he reflects on my words.

"I'm not an artist, so I've never looked at it this way," he admits. "But I like it. Your words, your passion, it's..."

He hesitates, looking at me with a mischievous smile.

"Beautiful," he finishes his sentence. "Honestly, it makes me want to fuck you."

I blush and avert my eyes from him as I giggle like a shy school girl.

"What a romantic you are, Mr. Abrams."

His eyes flicker with a dark promise.

"Come here," he orders - and I get up from my chair and obey his command.

CHAPTER XXXIII

Kingston

Elodie's eyes reflect the flames of the candles as she comes closer to me in cautious and slow steps. As always, she's completely calm on the outside while I know her insides are in turmoil. It's only her heaving chest that belies the excitement that my sudden change in demeanor causes for her.

She comes to a halt right next to my chair and I turn around, remaining seated while placing my hands on her behind and pulling her closer, my legs parting to give her room. She's wearing another dress I bought for her, a dark and very short cocktail dress with a laced hem. My hands travel across the curves of her ass, moving along the back side of her upper thighs until I reach the hem of her dress, pausing for a moment before my fingers move underneath the fabric. My intention was to pull down the pantyhose she's wearing underneath, but when my fingertips find the bare skin of her thighs, I realize that she's wearing stockings tonight.

I look up at her and see her smiling down at me, an expression of playful pride.

"You naughty girl," I whisper.

"You made me this way," she breathes back. "And I love it."

I get up from my chair and cause her to exclaim a sound of surprise when I lift her up in my arms, turning toward the hallway that leads to my bedroom.

"You're staying tonight," I tell her. "No ifs, ands, or buts."

She presses her lips together to keep herself from following her instinct to do just that, to reject my invitation. I won't let that happen, not tonight.

"And if you try to leave anyway," I say, as we walk through the door to my bedroom. "I'll just fuck you until you pass out in my arms."

She shrieks with delight when I throw her onto the bed, following right behind her, hovering over her beautiful body like a predator. I lean down, claiming her with a kiss, and she moans as she welcomes my lips. Our tongues intertwine hungrily, yearning for each other, seeking a closeness that only exists between the two of us.

"Take off my tie," I breathe in between our kisses.

She obeys and clumsily opens the knot of my tie as we dive into our next kiss. I didn't tell her to do so, but she continues by unbuttoning my shirt. When I break our kiss again and stare into her green eyes, she bites her lips apologetically.

"Please," she breathes, begging for me to allow her to undress me.

"Go ahead."

I grant her permission and her eyes flicker with joy when I sit up and allow her to take charge for just this moment. She sits up in front of me, claiming another kiss while her hands travel beneath the fabric of my shirt, feeling out the outline of my hard-earned muscles. The moan she lets out while caressing my buff chest drives me insane with need for her.

She removes my suit jacket and my shirt, leaving only the loosened tie around my neck, playfully yanking at it, while casting a cheeky smile up at me.

I shake my head, looking at her through narrow eyes.

"You are asking for trouble," I tell her.

Elodie smirks. "Am I?"

I push her back onto the sheets, grabbing her wrist and forcing her arms above her head, while she squirms beneath me, playfully trying to break free from my grip. Her struggle is half-hearted and when I take the tie from my neck while holding her hands in place, she stops moving completely, squealing with joy when I use the tie to fasten her hands together.

"Those hands better stay there," I warn her, before reaching behind her back to unzip her dress. I've envisioned taking her like this numerous times before, which is why I chose a strapless dress that can be pulled down even when her hands are forced above her head. I slowly pull the dress down her slim body, appreciating every inch as it is exposed in front of my eyes, until Elodie is lying before me, wearing nothing but her lacy underwear and the matching stockings. Such a good girl, looking so sinfully hot.

"You should wear this for your next performance," I say, as my hands travel along the inside of her thighs, causing her to shiver with lust and spreading her legs for me, more and more with every inch that I'm moving closer to her center.

"I'm not sure the audience would appreciate it as much as you do," she whispers, looking at me with a mischievous smile.

As beautiful as she looks, I want her naked, so I can tease her sensitive body. She arches her back when I unhook her bra, exposing her perky breasts and her hard nipples. I cup her boobs, pinching her nubs between my fingers before I place my lips around one of them, sucking and licking to tease her further. Elodie groans and squirms, flinching when I add little bites to my treatment, and sighing with bliss at the throbbing afterpain of my bites. She's lifting her hips, grinding against my leg with impatient lust.

I force her back down, bringing my hand beneath the fabric of her thong where I find the hot wetness of her arousal. She's dripping on my fingers when I caress her sensitive clit, sliding between her lips and carefully fingering her. Another moan escapes her lips when I add a second finger to spread her, while my tongue is still on her nipples, biting, sucking, teasing. It's almost too much for her. I notice her arms twitching, her hands threatening to move down to push me away and cover her agitated sensitive spots.

But she's a good girl, restraining herself as she remembers my command. She deserves a treat for that.

I pull down her thong, straightening up so I can enjoy the view of her in front of me, completely naked except for those deliciously sexy stockings, her legs spread apart and her heated body heaving with lust as she looks up at me with pleading eyes. Still, her tied up hands remain above her head, exactly where they belong.

I get up from the bed, her eyes following me as I get rid of my pants to free my throbbing erection. Her eyes widen with hunger when she sees it, and I come closer, stroking my length as my place myself between her legs.

She moans and squirms, spreading her legs further to invite me. "Please."

I move closer, teasing her wet entrance with the tip of my cock, searching for her eyes before I move any further.

Elodie nods. "It's okay."

She moves closer to me, and even if I wanted to, I wouldn't be able to resist at this point. I take her legs and lift them up while spreading her with my cock, fucking her bare for the first time and reveling in every inch as I push myself inside her. She moans as she takes all of me in, her arms flying up once again, threatening to move where they shouldn't be, but Elodie remembers just in time, her eyes closing shut as she restrains herself.

I fuck her like I've never fucked her before, ramming myself inside of her like a wild animal while she shrieks beneath me, accompanying every push with a released moan. Her passion is contagious, egging me on even more. I lean forward, my face close to hers while I continue to plunge inside her wet center, while her tight muscles tense around me. Her eyes meet mine, dazed with desire and I grab her arms, allowing her to move them down so they're wrapped around me. A smile flees across her face, and I can't help but kiss her. Elodie is still the only woman I've wanted to kiss while my cock is buried inside her, and I've accepted that things are different with her. She made me lose my conviction, she proved me wrong without ever trying.

When I heard others talk about love, I pitied them, called them fools for falling for such an idiotic illusion. I had no idea. This is what it feels like. A hunger that can never be assuaged, the desperate need to be close to a person, as close as possible. Even now I wish I could lose that last bittiness of distance that still seems to exist between us. Physically, I'm as close to Elodie right now as two people can possibly be, but I still want more.

I will always want more with her.

Her groans grow louder, more desperate, and her body is shaking beneath me, announcing her release. I want her to come, I want to see her explode with bliss while being this close to her.

"Come!" I edge her on. "Come, and look at me when you do!"

She wants to reply something, but her frenzy robs her of words. Instead, she lets out one last, hearty sigh, and I can feel her muscles clenching around my cock when she's overcome by waves of release. Instinct tells her to close her eyes, but she fights it to obey my wish and looks straight into my eyes. I can see everything in them. Her irises are widening, breathing with her throbbing orgasm as she loses herself in that staggering rapture.

Just before her release begins to fade, I join her in paradise, filling her as I reach my own climax with a brutality that's new to me. Elodie reacts to my orgasm as if it was her own, erupting in another wave of thrilling spasms, as she accompanies me over the edge.

We're breathing heavily, entangled in a close embrace after the euphoria dies down. I know this won't be the last one for tonight. When I told her that I'd fuck her until she passes out, I meant it. I'm not done with her, not for tonight, not ever. I will be inside of her again and again, and I will come closer to her, trying to overcome that last bit of distance between us.

She needs to hear it. I've been waiting for the right time and place, especially after I almost screwed it up with my outburst at the engagement party, when the words slipped out of my mouth without preparation. Even I wasn't ready for them then, but I am now.

"I love you, Elodie Hill," I whisper, reveling in the little chuckle and teary-eyed beam as she responds.

"I love you, too, Kingston Abrams."

Elodie

"**A**re you sure you're okay?" I ask again, leaning over to Kingston who has been nervously playing with the food on his plate for the entire evening. "You've hardly eaten anything."

"Yes, I'm fine," he insists, casting me a reassuring smile. "Stop worrying."

"Oh, I think it's sweet," Mrs. Abrams interjects. She's sitting opposite of us, her watchful eyes never missing a thing we say or do. "And she's right, Kingston. I've never seen you eat so little."

"Stressful week, that's all," Kingston tries to excuse himself.

"You asked for it," his father says, casting him a reproachful look. "I told you, being the CEO of such a huge company in that industry, it's no picnic."

"It's worth it," Kingston says, his tone as sharp as always when he speaks with his father.

Even after agreeing to let Kingston take over, despite him still being a bachelor, Mr. Abrams still hasn't forgiven him for what happened more than six months ago. The disastrous evening of the engagement party has left a dark mark on Kingston's relationship with his strict father, who knew about the lack of feelings in his son's engagement, but couldn't care less about it. For him, there's nothing wrong with a marriage being nothing more than a business arrangement, even though he didn't marry Kingston's mother for those reasons.

While she didn't come from a background as poor as mine, she's no Gloria Waldorf either and struggled through her entire time at Juilliard the same way I did. It's one of the reasons why she felt close to me from the beginning. She's the complete opposite of Mr. Abrams and has welcomed me with open arms from day one. If it wasn't for her, things would be a lot harder, and not only for me. She was the one who convinced her husband to give Kingston a chance at this CEO position, even without a bride at his side. His stubbornness is unmatched. I will never understand why it mattered so much to him that Kingston was tamed by marriage before he could take over the business, even though I do understand that his promiscuous ways weren't reassuring when it comes to his character, either.

The first time Kingston invited me to his parents' home as his girlfriend, I was met with welcoming arms by Mrs. Abrams and a stone-cold stare by Mr. Abrams. It was terribly awkward, and even now, when I think back on that evening months ago, I feel sick to the stomach. While we're still not on best terms with each other, things have gotten a lot better lately, and when we arrived tonight, Mr. Abrams even smiled at me. It was the same, warm smile that I'd usually just get from Kingston's mother.

"How are things going with you, dear?" she asks me across the table, trying to divert from the topic of family business, which I know she doesn't like to have discussed at the dinner table. "I heard you played for the Barringtons last week?"

"I did," I say. "It was a fundraiser event at the most beautiful venue, very well-attended. I don't think I've ever played for that many people before. They asked for a very classical arrangement, but gave me a lot of leeway for the composition of the program."

Mrs. Abrams smiled. "That must have been right up your alley."

"Yes, I enjoyed it a lot," I admit. "And I think they were happy, too."

"They were," Mrs. Abrams says, to my surprise. "I've talked to Mrs. Barrington, she was very pleased with your performance. You're making quite a name for yourself in our circles. People know about your classical expertise, and they appreciate it."

I blush at her nice words. It's always been hard for me to cope with compliments, but when they're coming from someone like Mrs. Abrams it appears to be extra difficult.

Kingston clears his throat next to me.

"If you don't mind, we'll have to leave soon," he says. "We don't want to be late for the concert."

His parents both look at him, nodding with understanding.

"Yes, sure," Mrs. Abrams says, casting a warm smile in my direction. "The concert."

I smile back, slightly confused. For some reason, Mrs. Abrams has been extra warm and friendly tonight, and even Mr. Abrams seems to be affected by it. He's smiling at us, too.

We say our goodbyes and I'm surprised to see a black limousine waiting for us outside.

"You're not driving?" I ask Kingston as he opens the door for me.

"I wanted to have a drink with dinner," he says, as if that's ever been an excuse for him before. "And another on our way to the concert."

Even after being with him for half a year and being exposed to the luxuries that his wealth can afford, I'm still blown away by the limousine's inside decor.

"Wow," I gasp, sounding like child.

Kingston chuckles and proceeds to open a bottle of champagne for us while I hold the flutes for him to fill.

"Why so fancy tonight?" I ask him as we clink glasses. "I thought the concert was surprise enough. Scriabin, Ravel, Chopin - the program is amazing!"

Kingston smiles at me, looking as handsome as always in his navy blue suit that goes so well with his dark hair.

"Why must there be an occasion?" he asks. "You should be used to me wanting to spoil you."

"I'll never get used to that," I whisper. "Never."

The drive to Carnegie Hall is way too short, and even though I'm looking forward to the concert, I'm almost sorry to leave that luxurious limousine when we arrive.

Kingston acts as the perfect gentleman, except when he grabs my ass while we're walking inside, reminding me of his domineering nature in bed for just a second. Even after all these months together, a touch like this still sends electrifying shivers through my entire body.

We leave our coats at the cloakroom, and while the clerk is handling my coat, Kingston taps me on the arm from the side.

"Could you wait here for a moment," he says. "I need to go the bathroom real quick."

I nod. "Sure."

He winks at me. "Don't get kidnapped, beautiful."

My eyes follow him as he walks away, a confused expression on my face. He's acting strangely tonight, and I wonder if I should worry about him. Is the stress at work too much? I've also never seen him drink this much champagne in such a short amount of time. He emptied two glasses on our short drive here, while I barely finished my first.

We're very early and still have a lot of time to pass until the concert starts. This also explains why there aren't many other people around as I wait for Kingston to return. Minutes pass without him showing up again, and just as I begin to worry, I'm approached by one of the young ushers.

"Miss Hill?" he asks.

I look at him, instantly frightened that something must've happened to Kingston. "Yes?"

"If you'd please follow me," he says. "I am to bring you to your seat."

"Uh... no, I'm waiting for my boyfriend to-"

"Mr. Abrams asked me to get you," the usher says. "He's waiting for you."

I furl my eyebrows, but follow him through the hallway. What the hell is going on here? Why didn't Kingston just come back for me like he said he would? He told me not to get kidnapped, and now this?

The usher passes every door that leads to the main seating area of the auditorium, and we're coming closer to the stage with every step. I want to stop him and tell him that I doubt that this is where our seats are, but when he leads me through a door that clearly states 'staff only', I'm beginning to think that something strange is going on.

"Why are we here?" I ask him. "Where is Kingston?"

I'm starting to worry. How do I know this really is an usher? What if this man is a criminal who just put on a uniform to fool me and who's about to kidnap me for real? Maybe Kingston was worried about something like this happening? Could that be it?

Or is it just my imagination running wild?

"Please," the usher says after we've crossed another, much smaller and darker hallway. He's opening another door, beckoning for me to walk through.

I hesitate. "Why-"

"Please, Miss Hill," he repeats, winking at me. "Have a wonderful evening."

I cast him another confused look, but follow his gesture, walking through the door - and right into the dark.

"What-"

I'm interrupted by the door closing behind me, and surrounded by complete darkness. Just very faint lights here and there reveal enough for me to see that I must be inside the giant Stern Auditorium, standing directly next to the stage.

"Hello?" I ask, my voice echoing through the darkness.

I jump in fright when I hear a familiar c-sharp minor chord coming from my left, and almost simultaneously, a warm spotlight is turned on, illuminating the stage where a song is played on a grand piano.

And Kingston is sitting on the bench, partly hidden in the dark as he plays the first few, soft tunes of my favorite Nocturne written by Chopin.

It's the Nocturne I played for him on the day we first talked to each other in private.

I walk toward the stage, realizing that it is covered in red roses as I take the steps that lead up to it. The Nocturne is no easy piece to play and it must have taken Kingston a lot of effort to be able to perform it at all. His notes are as gentle and slow as they should be during the opening of the piece. He's not always hitting the rhythm as the song dictates, but touching just the right chord in my heart.

I can't believe he put this much work into this. For me.

The roses are covering the floor, just leaving a small path that leads to the center of the stage, illuminated by the light. I follow the path and just as I reach the center of the spotlight, Kingston looks up from the keys, finishing a few more tunes before he lets the song fade away in melancholic chords.

He gets up and walks toward me, displaying a smile on his face that I've never seen before.

He seems nervous, shy even.

I stare at him, dumbfounded as my heart is about to jump out of my breast and the last chord of the Nocturne is still resonating through my heart.

"Kingston," I breathe. "How did you..."

He places his index finger on his lips, beckoning me to hush.

"I wanted to know what it's like," he says. "This way of expression, to share your feelings with music. And I wanted *you* to know what it's like to be on the receiving end. You deserve to be serenaded, even if it's by a philistine like me."

I shake my head, the lump in my throat threatening to choke me, as Kingston steps closer until he's standing right in front of me.

"About half a year ago, I was meant to be tamed," he says. "And even though they picked the wrong woman to make me a man, I'm glad I was forced to go through with it as far as we did. Because otherwise, I would never have met you, Elodie."

He pauses, his eyes fixated on mine while I try my best not to choke on the tears that are threatening to make an appearance.

"You never tried to tame me," he continues. "And yet, you did. You made me chase you. You were the forbidden fruit I couldn't taste enough. And you taste just as delicious now that I no longer have to hide you. And I'm ready for more, for a new kind of taste."

My heart skips a beat at his words.

That's when he does it. Kingston Abrams goes down on his knee in front of me, producing a small jewelry box from the inside pocket of his suit jacket.

"I want to taste you when you're legally mine. Every single day. Forever," he says, opening the jewelry box, presenting a beautiful diamond ring with an elegant yet simple cathedral setting.

"Elodie Hill, will you do me the honor of becoming my wife?"

I know I'm not the first woman to be too choked up for a proper reply to this question, but I still find it necessary to shower him with kisses after I sink down on my knees, falling right into his strong arms, just to make sure that he knows how much I love him, and how much I want him.

Because, how could I not?

The End

ABOUT THE AUTHOR

Linnea May loves to read and write about strong alpha men with loaded bank accounts and skeletons in their closets. Her heroes are as sexy and beautiful as they are broken - only to be fixed by the smart & captivating heroines who cross their paths.

KEEP IN TOUCH

Sign up to my mailing list to get the latest news about new book releases and to get your FREE short story: **"Anniversary,"** a steamy scene with the protagonists of my other BDSM Romance novel *I Am Yours.*

Linnea's Newsletter:
http://eepurl.com/bb5Z45

Linnea's Author Page:
https://www.amazon.com/Linnea-May/e/B00RS8VDI0

Made in the USA
Charleston, SC
25 January 2017